GRANNY'S TEACAKES, GRAB'LED 'TATERS, AND A GILLION TWICE-TOLD TALES

Faye Brown

Illustrations by Trille Brown

Printed by CAMCO Printing, Northport, AL
Elizabeth Renicks, Production Editor

Published by
POT LIKKER PRESS
Faye Brown
Rt. 2 Box 440
Moundville, AL 35474

Faye Brown is a noted humorist, motivator, and inspirational speaker. References available. Contact her for speaking engagements. Tel. (205) 371-6316, or by mail:

Faye Brown
Rt. 2, Bx 440
Moundville, AL 35474

First Printing. 1994
ISBN- 0-9642397-0-1

Printed in the United States of America

DEDICATED TO:

Trillie Brown,
my sister,
my friend,
without whose marvelous illustrations
my books would have been nothing.

And to my beloved husband, Joe Brown,
without whose help my books would never
have been.

WHAT FOLKS ARE SAYING:

"I've shared many of Faye's wonderful books for gifts. It's so refreshing to know such a lovely writer who shares the wonderful times as well as the trials."

Elizabeth Cooper, Pulaski, TN

"I re-live my life through Faye's writings. I thank her for writing so much of my history."

Velma Morgan, Cave Spg, GA

"Faye's stories remind me how simple, good,—and sometimes, hard life can be. And how important family is, or should be, to us."

Meredith King, Thomson, GA

"I have gotten Faye's books for my grandchildren to read and enjoy..she has written "the story of my life" which the young ones wanted me to write."

Helen Jameson, Clarksville, GA

"Never have I had so much enjoyment going back to my childhood and The Depression Days as when reading Faye's books."

Noreen Southerland, Waynesburg, KY

"Faye's stories remind me of growing up in rural Oklahoma."

Marsha Chandler, Two Egg, FL.

"Through Faye's stories I re-live my childhood on a Missouri hill farm during the Great Depression."

Freda Madison, Jackson, MO.

Table of Contents

LEGEND: In these recipes the following terms are abbreviated.

C = cup	gal = gallon
qt = quart	T = Tablespoon
tsp = teaspoon	

Unless otherwise indicated, the terms "flour" or "meal" indicate "plain."

Comin' Up 'Terek'ly . . .

More great stories from Faye Brown! Plus some mighty fine eatin' from lotta yer neighbors. Course'n iffen ye ain't hungry don't go and skip the vittle parts, 'cause tucked all among 'em is some dandy tales.

"Older readers of GRANNY'S TEACAKES, GRAB'LED 'TATERS, AND A GILLION TWICE-TOLD TALES will nod their heads, smile and whisper to themselves, "Yes, I remember . . . " as each story stirs a flood of recollections. Young readers will likely find it hard to believe that growing up in rural Alabama could have been so much fun back in "olden times," but they'll grieve over the pleasures they've missed."
— Kathryn Tucker Windham,
Historian, Storyteller,
and Author of <u>13 Alabama Ghosts and Jeffrey</u>, and many other books
Selma, AL

We Needed The New Year's Black-Eyed-Peas-Luck

Now-a-days the luck most hoped for on New Year's is "that your favorite team will win in a bowl game." When I was a skinny kid living off red-dirt tenant farming, we felt our destiny for the entire year was sealed by the eating of black-eyed peas on New Year's day. And the fact that we were God-fearing, Bible-believing fundamentalists never seemed contradictory to our time-honored, unflinching tradition of cooking and eating the symbolic peas the first day of every new year.

Many folks thought, like my little brother, that for your good fortune to hold out you had to eat one pea for every day of the upcoming year. It took a long time for an eight-year-old to count out that many of the legumes. But little Donald was determined to have a good, happy day every day of the year that had just been born. And so he counted them out... "one...twenty...ninety-nine...three hundred sixty...THREE HUNDRED SIXTY-FIVE!" That was it; he had his peas parceled out!

And now for the eating of the huge plateful of the dark, swollen peas. But hadn't the peas been cooked by Grandma and seasoned deliciously with hog jowl raised, slaughtered, and smoked by Grandpa Shirley? And wasn't there plenty of hot cracklin' cornbread to go along with the peas? Why, there'd be no problem at all, Donald felt, in guaranteeing his good fortune by reducing the pea pile to naught. And, if worse-came-to-worse, he could save part of the peas for his suppertime meal. It just depended on them being consumed before the grandfather clock in the front room struck midnight and ushered in January 2. And so with great optimism little Donald began eating his peas, and ensuring his good luck.

That New Year's Day, so many years ago, brought fresh light to me regarding the tradi-

tion of peas on January 1. As my family and I
sat up and down that long, roughly hewn table
in my Grandma's kitchen (casting occasional
glances toward Donald and his diminishing
heap)—well, my Grandma and my Grandpa
Shirley shared 'pea beliefs' held firmly by
Grandpa's five sisters: Tennessee, Alabama,
Louisiana, Cherokee, and—the oddly named
one, Pearly Elizabeth.

Alabama (my Great Aunt Bama), reportedly, felt the peas symbolized pennies and the
more you ate on New Year's Day, the more
pennies would come your way in the following
year.

Tennessee (Aunt Tenny) was convinced
that each pea you ate ensured you of earning
that many dollars within the year. Grandpa
quoted her. "She'd say she'd seen it work; had
a neighbor once who ate a thousand peas on
January the First. That year he had a bumper
cotton crop and cleared exactly $1,000 dol-
lars!"

"Of course, she maintained," Papa added,
"you gotta be sure the peas are dried one.
Canned peas aren't worth a hoot toward getting wealth."

Louisiana (Aunt Lou), it seems, stood

firm that "the black-eyed peas will bring you no luck a'tall 'less'n you put lots of hot pepper sauce on them and eat them without tears coming into your eyes."

Cherokee (Aunt Cherry) vowed that "the longer you soak your peas the longer your luck extends," my Grandma Shirley recalled. "So she soaked hers two, three days instead of overnight like I do."

And the one with the mis-fit name, Pearly Elizabeth (the one after whom my Mama was named Pearlie)—"Well, Aunt 'Lizzie," Grandpa told, "will argue till her death that 'for the New Year's peas to bring luck your way you also have to eat a fair-sized slice of Hog's Head Cheese (Souse Meat) with them.' "

When our heads were filled with the new knowledge, and Donald's plate was empty (and his heart was filled with great hope), we hitched up the team and headed home from Grandpa's on that long-ago January 1.

Since we had stayed overnight with our grandparents and had missed our traditional 'serenading of the neighbors' the previous night, we decided we should do it, belatedly, when dark crept in that day. Daddy, tired from the trip, decided we kids were "grown enough" to take the coal oil lantern and go it alone.

After a night of fun we started home. As we marched along the muddy dirt road ringing the cow bells, Mr. Lowe's huge old bull got confused in the darkness of the night. Perhaps he mistook us for a strange cow, a potential lover. Or maybe it was the beautiful new red overcoat I was wearing, reflecting in the moonlight. (Mama had sewn it so handsomely I felt it shined all by itself.)

But whatever incited the monstrous bull— Bill held the lantern high just in time to see him snort, paw the ground, and come charging—taking the rotten pasture fence posts and the rusted barbed wire with him—heading full-blast down the road toward our troupe of eight kids, mostly small.

Maybe it was the strength from the peas' protein that helped us travel faster than the blazing string ball we often threw while celebrating the New Years' beginnings. But the most celebrating we did that particular year, and perhaps the most for all time, was the celebrating we did once we scrambled to safety inside our kitchen door, just ahead of that raging bull. Celebrating with Little Donald shouting, "WHEW! That was good, black-eyed-peas-luck!" We all hugged him, grateful he'd eaten that huge plate of peas. The Good Lord knew we needed that luck!

When Mama Tied Her Apron Strings

The endless possibilities made my heart flip-flop every morning. As Mama stood at the foot of my bed calling me to face each childhood day, she'd always be tying her apron strings. I now realize that Mama's aprons were just fabric coverings which she added over her worn house dresses. But long ago they seemed more magical than the cape on Superman in my brother's comic book; they were mystical garments whose varied uses only a day would tell.

Mama's apron met a stern test at the kitchen cabinet and the cook stove. For there it's full skirt and bibbed top were called upon to catch grease popping from the ham or batter from the flap jacks. And extra flour from the gingerbread, the chicken dumplings, or the pie crusts was poofed upon it. Wet hands, washed free of sticky dough and needed quickly to stir the stew, were dried with the handy garment's edge.

We older siblings would prepare to meet the rolling store; Mama'd carefully take a little money from her apron pocket. "Two Big Red tablets, sugar, and some tobacco for your Daddy; what's left in stick candy," she'd smile. Then quickly she'd turn to Sue—whose heart was broken to be left behind—and she'd gently wipe the baby's tears on her coverall, the worn garment which faintly read "6-8-4" in blue.

Springtime we'd be in the garden as the morning sun rose higher. Mama'd be showing us how to train the little runners on the pole beans, how to start them on their journey up the strings. Then we'd hear her shout, "Well, I'll declare! This lettuce is plenty big for a mess. And the radishes and onions are raring, too." Pretty soon she'd leave the garden with her apron-turned-basket brimming over with the spring's first bounty.

A short while later we'd troop toward the hen house. We'd sashay by the corn crib for a couple ears of corn which Mama'd shell into her tied-up apron-pail. I'd keep my distance as the flogging settin' hen left her nest for the food. Soon I'd hear my courageous Mama squeal, "They've hatched!" Then, "Oh, you bad, bad momma, you've injured your babies."

The fantastic apron instantly changed into an ambulance. It rushed the struggling biddies to a quickly-improvised high-risk nursery, a box with clean rags underneath the warm woodstove. Once the little doodies were breathing easier Mama'd say, " 'Spect I better tie on a clean apron 'fore I get dinner." Then once again my heart beat faster just to see her hands behind her back, tying together her enchanting apron strings.

Afternoons sometimes found us visiting Miss Mamie. Once welcomed properly, we children would play quietly. Mama'd take needle, thread, and thimble from her knock-about apron pocket.

While the neighbors talked, Mama'd patch a pair of overalls for little Bill. Then home we'd head, sweet potatoes from Miss Mamie's hill caught up in my Mama's apron skirt.

If primroses were blooming beside the gravel road we'd skip along and pick a few for Mama. She'd glow and add them to the 'taters; the spacious apron became a vase.

The ever'day aprons which Mama tied on were often sewn quickly from the rough guano sacks; I had my first sewing machine lessons while making them. Pretty floral feedsacks were sometimes spared for a knock-about apron for my Mom; these were fashioned more cautiously. The finest stitches Mama could make, however, and even bits of lace, were used when making Sunday aprons. It was important that they look nice since they were quickly donned over church dresses when the preachers came for dinner.

Mama used her aprons in so many ways. They became bowls; she'd shell peas and butterbeans in their yard-wide tails. In them she would transport eggs from the hen house or from a stolen nest which she located in the woods while out for a little walk on Sunday afternoon.

She would take off her apron and tie it around a sick baby's head if they were caught unexpectedly in a downpour. Or if the baby wet its hippin' while she washed at the spring, Mama'd lay the little one gently across her lap and sacrifice her apron, folding and pinning it to cover the small bare bottom.

When we came to the table to eat Mama'd put a couple of big cattylogs into the bottom of a straight chair. Then she'd place a toddler thereon and, lastly, tie the young child securely into the chair, again using her versatile apron.

Mama's sisters—Jessie, Zula, Margaret, and Bert— would all come to visit—plus their husbands and a passel o' younguns. Before long the womenfolk would be cooking up a storm in the kitchen, and the wonderful smells would be drifting outside. Then the flies would come flocking in, especially as we kids ran in and out, leaving the makeshift screen door ajar. When this happened Mama and her sisters took off their aprons and declared war on the flies. While one of the Shirley girls stood near the door to open and close it, the others stationed themselves in the furthermost corners of the room. They began to swish and pop their aprons back and forth, scaring the flies in their wake. The ladies flapped and flopped the aprons until they had a big drove of the insects near the exit. The door was then flung open and a batch of them driven out. It would then be decent in the kitchen for about an hour. Then the room would again be thick with the pesky flies and the womenfolk would, once more, take off their handy aprons and have another big "fly drive."

If Mama caught a stray chicken or a dog on either the front or the back porch she'd begin shooing and scaring them away with the bottom part of her apron in a rapid flight. I sometimes felt as if Mama's apron was part of the reason we were respectable folk, that it helped give us dignity, separate us—though poor we were—from "pore white trash."

Yes, the uses to which Mama put her aprons excited me when I was a kid. So whenever she began, early 'a morning, tying on her apron strings my mind started whirling, wondering just what she'd use the cover-up for during that day. You see—my Mama's apron strings, when tied, were not the kind that bound her offsprings to her. They were never ones to restrict her children's growth nor their freedom to expand. Instead the ties held a simple fabric shield around her body; around her big, wise heart.

Mama's now well past her four-score years and I'm past my three but whenever I go to visit and she's tying on an apron I still get an excited flutter. My mind flits back to a cotton patch where my young brothers, sisters, and I were picking scrap cotton for a little Christmas cash. My pricked hands were almost in blood, my back was frozen in a U-shape, and hunger pangs were telling me that I was "soon to PASS." Then Mama arrived, just like the angel of mercy that came to feed old Elijah when he was starving and down-and-out. Mama thrust her hands into her ample apron pockets and brought forth abundantly food that saved the body and sustained the soul, warm teacakes wrapped in waxed paper and smelling deliciously of Granny's ginger.

Grandpa Didn't
Need A Microchip
For Tracking Bees

The evening news just reported the development of a tiny computer chip which has the potential for tracking the unwelcome killer bees. Seems the device, weighing about the same as a grain of sand, is attached to captured bees' midsections to monitor their base stations and their future movements. Now my Grandpa Shirley didn't have today's sophisticated microchips to help him with tracking honey bees back to their trees years ago, but, according to his son, he actually had no need of them. (Seems he loved honey and was always trying to locate some. Felt that maybe when Isaiah the Prophet was writing about the coming Messiah being one that would eat 'butter and honey' so he would know to refuse evil and choose good—felt that perhaps God meant all men to follow the same route.)

"He was a good 'un at it (tracking bees)," my Uncle Vic recounted recently. Papa'd walk up and down branches (of water) in early spring. He'd find 'em (the bees) waterin' and set in a'watchin' 'em. When he (the bee) gits up from waterin' he makes a beeline for his hive. Now when they're feedin' on flowers it's different—then they go from one t' nother'n and you can't course 'em— but when they're a'waterin'— well, Papa'd watch 'em when they got up from waterin'...AND HE COULD SEE ONE A HALF MILE OFF....Sometimes he'd stand up on top of the hill above the branch and watch where they went after topping the hill from the water. And sometimes I've seen him lay out old honey or put sweetened water in a saucer—put the bait out on a stump and watch the bees leaving for the hive with the sweetenin'," my Mama's only brother told.

Some other old timers have also explained

why it's a difficult task to locate a tree where
wild bees are storing up honey for the next
winter. "Wild bees're smart and you've gotta be
too, if'n you wanta beat 'em at their own game.
After bees git their sweetenin' they're gonna go
'round 'n 'round, higher 'n higher, before they
head straight for their home," one feller offered, free-of-charge. "And you've gotta have a
keen eye and stick with it (watching and tracking the bees) if you wanta enjoy that honey."

Once my Grandpa had activated his built-
in radar, then covered the ground (with his
long legs and his huge feet)... once he had
found the bee tree, being the Christian gent
that he was.... Well, then he'd check it out,
making sure noone else had found and marked
the tree previously. If unclaimed, he'd quickly
make an "X" on it and then approach the land
owner about cutting the tree for its honey and
for the bees. And, according to my Uncle Vic,
"Most land owners back then were willing for
you to cut the tree. They had more timber than
they could use and they were obliging to their
neighbors."

When asked what happened if someone
cut a tree that had been claimed earlier, my
Uncle Vic related, "Sometimes a'body'd get a

whuppin' about it if they cut one that was already marked. But most folks honored the marks on bee trees."

"Papa would cut the trees in April, May, or sometimes early June—never later. For one thing, the honey was best at that time. And the bees would swarm (from their original tree) into a bee 'gum', or hive, that we brought for that purpose. Usually we wanted the bees more'n we wanted the honey," my Uncle declared. "Truth is, sometimes we wouldn't get that much honey from the bee trees. Seems most of 'em had more of that old 'bee bread' than they did good honey."

"But there was times," Vic continued, "when there was lots of honey. Once we were fishing up on North River— a whole bunch of us, Papa and me and other men. Papa found a bee tree and we got permission and cut it before dark the same day. Everybody ate all they could hold, got all their buckets full, and then we filled a wash tub full and toted it home."

But as my uncle, who now enjoys keeping bees in a modernized manner,—as he remembers it, "Cutting a bee tree was some of the hardest, roughest work I've ever done. Back then there was no bought veils —so you had a choice. You could either wrap yourself up in old cheese cloths and such—and then let the bees get up underneath the cloths—or you could just let those wild bees eat you up to begin with. AND THEY'D DO IT, TOO. Now I'll have to admit—Papa was rough on bees. When he'd be smoking 'em out—and if they started getting rowdy—well, he'd put the smoke too close to 'em, almost burn 'em up. You gotta be easy with bees."

Continuing, Vic explained. "Back then we used old rags and pieces of cotton quilts to smoke 'em. We'd roll 'em up, set 'em afire, wave 'em around and git 'em a'smokin' good. And then Papa'd blow the smoke (with his mouth) into their hole."

In addition to input from the maternal side of my family, my Daddy's brothers, Gray and Ferman, have also added to my "bee-tree-knowledge.' Gray said he could certainly re-member cutting the trees "and gettin' stung like the dickens. We just cut 'em in our shirt sleeves, usually, without veils. They (the bees) won't stay around that smoke much—they'll go back up in there where the honey is, but a few outsiders are out there to stay and if you don't watch THEY'LL GIT YE. When I'd fight at 'em they'd sting the douse outta me!"

My Uncle Ferman shared one outstanding bee tree story with me. "In the hog pasture there was a little old bay (tree). Searcy found it and they'uz gonna rob it. Well, Timmons, he jest run in there like he wuz gonna catch a squirrel and them thangs just WROPPED HIM UP! He come out a'knocking with both hands! I hollered, 'YOU WAIT'LL I GIT MY SMOKE FIXED, I'LL HELP YE.' I bet they'uz a dozen stung 'im." Overhearing the telling, my Uncle Gray enlarged, "WHY, I SPECT THEY'UZ MORE LIKE FORTY GOT IM, IF THEY'UZ ONE!"

When asked how much honey he'd seen come from bee trees, Uncle Ferman quipped, "Gen'lly they ain't that much. But they cut one above Choyce Dyer's and I bet they got a tub full outta it. I know Paw and ole man John Robertson and Ruff Parker helped cut it. It was Andrew Anderson's tree. He'd hunted and hunted fer it, him and Mr. Whit Shelton. Mr. Whit had hunted fer it a month, nearabout. And it wuz a big tall pine—they build in pines sometimes. I bet we got a wash tub full outta it! They went and cut it—they shouldna' done it. I know I was small but Mr. John said, 'Billy,

I'll back you outta cuttin' Andrew's bee tree.'
And he said, 'Naw you won't either!' So they got
the crosscut saw and the ax and went and cut
it one Sunday e'enin...Law, we filled every
bucket we had and it run down the hill, I bet
ten foot—the honey did—where the tree busted
when it fell."

"Sometimes the bees'd build right at the
ground and you could 'saw in' down there, but
gen'lly they'd build higher up," my Daddy's
baby brother kept packing into my store of bee
information. "We'd git bees whenever they'd
swarm in the sprang (spring). We'd build a new
gum—a section from a hollow gum tree. And
save some of the swarms. They gen'lly swarmed
every spring; a new bunch come in. You can git
'em to settle by beatin' on a plow or ringing a
bell. I thought they'uz gonna a swarm of 'em
settle on my mule one time. We'uz plowing over
in that red field over there. They come over and
they'uz so low down I thought fer sure they'uz
gonna settle on that mule.But they went on
and got in Mr. Vic's (Elmore's) peach tree."

(I could relate to my uncle's story here.
One spring in the early 1970s a swarm settled
on the end of our brick house, in a crowded
subdivision. By the time the summoned fire

department had arrived to help solve my dilemma—well, the bees had departed—en masse—for parts unknown.)

"Yep, you have to have a good eye to 'sight 'em when you're looking for a tree," testified my Uncle Ferman who said that he'd "helped rob a-many-a-bee-tree. That honey wuz real 'portent to us; honey and blue cane and sorgham syrup was about all we had to sweeten with during WW I and during The Depression. I'll tell ye—Maw could sure make some good teacakes with that honey. And we needed a good amount on hands fer colds in the winter; alluz mixed honey with that bitter alum fer cough sirup. And Maw used that beeswax (from the honeycomb) fer smoothin' up her flat irons when she'uz ironing up our thangs t'wear t'meetin'."

Yep, oldtimers like my uncles can teach us younger generation much about the ways of nature and about co-existing peacefully with God's wonderful creations. And just as my Grandpa's early training gave him a keen eye to aid in tracking bees without a modern-microchip-tracking-device— even so my friend Raymond's early-learned-lesson in regard to insects has stuck with him through life.

Seems Raymond's hard lesson came about this way: He and his dad, Mr. Ed Fields, were out clearing a ditch bank of its saplings and shrubs one hot summer day. Mr. Ed, spying a huge wasp nest on one of the small trees advised his son, "Let's pick up our hoes and move carefully around this nest of fierce looking red wasps." Nine-year-old mischievous Raymond couldn't resist the temptation for what he thought'd be fun. So as he ran by the dangerous area he poked his hoe into the nest—and then he fairly flew! Unaware of the boy's actions, Raymond's dad was soon covered up with the angry insects; he realized that a lot of wasp stings can be terribly painful—even more painful than the multitude of wild honey bee stings he had previously experienced.—AND, a little later that same afternoon—the story goes—Raymond had to learn the hard lesson that disobedience can result in a limb thrashing which is perhaps more painful that either honey bee or wasp stings. (Just how Mr. Ed's wasp stings would've stacked up with killer bee stings is unsure; perhaps we'll never need to know if they keep tracking them with the little microchip implants.)

"Father Smile On Us In Tender

Mercies And Make

Us Thankful For

These Blessings

And All Other

Blessings, For

Your Name's Sake

Alone We Ask This All. Amen."

My Daddy, Ira W. Porter, always prayed the above words of grace before we partook of a family meal. It mattered not if it were a summer Sunday and we were around a table spread lavishly for the visiting preachers—with fried chicken, creamed potatoes, gravy, hot biscuits, cut-off corn, fried okra, peas, hot cornbread, and fried apple pies a'waiting. Or if it were a freezing cold night and we were just huddled around the front room fireplace about to partake of a simple meal of sorgham syrup and hot flapjacks.

Yes, regardless of the table fare or circumstances no change was made in the "saying of grace" by Daddy. We could have been about to eat when a neighbor came rushing to the door to say that his mules were running away, or the radio could have blared out that WW II had just ended —and Daddy would have said, "I'll be along 'tereck'ly," or "Turn off that infernal radio," then expected each of us to quietly and reverently bow our heads while he intoned, "FATHER SMILE ON US...."

Regardless of how hungry, how tired, how rushed to be off to a party... we knew to not extend a hand for a morsel of food until after Daddy had prayed. His acknowledgement, at mealtime, of the Almighty's provision, I think, made us aware of His part even in making sure there were cold 'taters to eat in the afternoons as we rushed with one toward the cotton patch, silently thankful.

And Daddy's recognition, in his place as head-of-the-household, of God's goodness has continued to influence his eight living children more than three decades after his homegoing.

Spic-A-Bat And Other Breakfast Doin's

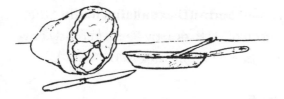

(Spic-A-Bat Gravy)

The One Thing that came close to being my Daddy's favorite thing in all the world was Spic-a-bat gravy, plus the fried country-cured ham from which it was derived. Daddy would've thought we "had arrived" if we had ever managed to hang enough hams into the smoke house to provide these two delicacies all year round. Here's the way to make that Spic-A-Bat Gravy:

Take cured ham from the smokehouse. Cut off the end for cooking in the dried butterbeans, then slice off several of the good slices, about 1/2-3/4 inches thick. Put a spoonful or two of grease in a skillet. Cook the ham slowly, turning over a time or two. Take the ham out and put on the end of the platter where you've placed the just-fried sunnyside-up eggs. Add about 1/2 cup of water (some folks use coffee instead of water) to the skillet, put the lid on and let it sort of 'melt' the good smoked flavor and all that salt that has browned in the bottom of the skillet. Remove lid and let part of the liquid evaporate. Serve piping hot; just spoon onto and soak a 'Cathead' (the name my Daddy used to refer to a very large biscuit)—onto a biscuit which has been broken open on your plate. Then eat quickly before the grease has time to congeal in the frigid room. (To answer your thought question: "No, my Daddy didn't die from, nor ever have, high blood pressure from the salt nor heart disease from the fat.")

FRIED CHICKEN

Yep—that's right. Fried chicken for breakfast. In the spring of the year when Mama had grown off a 'hunderd or so 'broilers' (young roosters), we sometimes had a Sunday morning treat of Fried Chicken. This meant that Mama rose very early, killed, scalded, picked the feathers off of, singed, cut up, then fried the best parts of two chickens—enough for one piece each. She put the bony pieces on to simmer and later added dumplings for the

noonday meal. Most
often, however, the
fried chicken AND the
dumplings were served
at Sunday Dinner,
when the preacher or
other company came.

1 frying chicken, about 2-2 1/2 lb.

(Be sure and cut up so you will have a "pulley
bone" to pull, so the younguns will know who's
gonna get married first and who's gonna have
the purttiest house.)

3/4 C flour;

salt; pepper, if desired (Mama didn't use)

lard (or vegetable oil)

Sprinkle the chicken pieces lightly with
salt. Roll them around in the flour until coated.
Heat about 2, 3 inches of lard (or vegetable oil)
in a skillet. Add chicken. Brown one side, turn
and then reduce heat and cover skillet. Cook
about 20 minutes, turning chicken when it is
browned. Check occasionally to make sure it's
not burning. Finally, remove the top and cook
additional 5 minutes, 'crisping' the chicken.
Remove onto plate.

"Tip: Put the liver and gizzard in last. And
watch out for 'em; they will pop grease onto ye

and burn the dickens out of ye."
(Gravy may be made from the browned bits left in pan as directed in the recipe for Salt Pork and Gravy, following.)

SALT PORK AND GRAVY

Agnes Anders, Northport, AL

1 pound salt pork	*Flour*
1 pint milk	*Salt and pepper*
Pure lard (or shortening) for frying	

Slice pork thin. Place in cold water and let stand 1 hour. Drain and dry. (Zelda Lawrence of Coker, AL said her Mama soaked her slices of streak-o-lean in buttermilk, overnight, then drained and fried—always, in pure lard.) Dip each piece into flour and fry in hot grease until crisp.

FOR MILK GRAVY: Drain off all but 2 table-spoons of fat and stir in 2 tablespoons of flour. Cook 2 minutes, stirring well. Reduce heat and add milk slowly. Cook until thickened. Add salt and pepper to taste. Pour over hot biscuits. YUM-YUM!!

Edna Fikes of Coker, AL says they rolled either salt pork or bacon in flour, then fried. They, like my Mama, added flour and WATER to some of the leftover grease, making 'Sawmill

Gravy.'

To make TOMATO GRAVY by Milk Gravy recipe, reduce the amount of milk and add either fresh or canned tomatoes (chopped or mashed). My Mama made tomato gravy often during summertime; it'll beat the tar outta the modern Hardee's "gravy with biscuits."

Laverne Poole of Linden, AL says they called the salt pork 'Tennessee Chicken' and soaked the slices one hour in HOT WATER, not cold. Then they sprinkled with hot pepper before dredging in flour and frying; being careful to always keep the slices pressed flat while frying, for even cooking . She attests it is "among the best tried and true hard-times food."

OLD FASHIONED SOUSE MEAT
(or PRESS MEAT)

Opal Broughton, Northport, AL

Cook the pig's head and feet until tender. Separate the skin and bones, leaving the good meat. Mix with salt, sage and a small amount of vinegar. (Some folks like to add black pepper or 2, 3 finely-chopped red pepper pods.) Mix by hand very thoroughly. Place in a large bowl. Place a plate on top of the meat. Place a heavy object on top of the bowl, heavy enough to press the meat downward and mold it. The heavy object should also help to squeeze some of the fat out of the meat.

After Souse is molded it can be sliced for breakfast, lunch or supper. Good eating any-time, but especially if served with collards for dinner.

GRANDMA'S LIVER PUDDING
Josephine Usher, McCall, SC

1 hog liver	1/3 hog head
1 1/2 cups corn meal	dash red pepper
3 large onions	2 tsp black pepper
1 1/2 C liquid	2 T salt
3/4 tsp sage	

Boil liver and hog head until tender. Brown meal in oven until lightly toasted. Grind all ingredients in meat grinder. Add season-ings. Josephine says, "Grandma patted hers into pans, then kept chilled in the pantry on freezing winter days. She sliced and served cold or heated. Today I pat into rolls, approxi-mately 1" x 3", wrap in plastic wrap and refrigerate. This freezes well also. Delicious served with grits for breakfast or supper around the fireplace. (Modern suggestion: Serve as a snack on saltine crackers.)"

Ross Ward from Charleston, SC said when he was young his folks added cooked rice to the "hog pudding." They scraped, skinned, and washed the large intestine and stuffed the pudding therein. The small intestine was saved for stuffing the sausage.

CALVES' FEET JELLY

Annie Northen, Shreveport, LA

**Faye's Note: Annie's mother-in-law must be "turning over in her grave." Annie took me so seriously about sending some old recipes until she literally "tore two pages from a 1892 cookbook which had belonged to her mother-in-law." Here's the recipe, as written and punctuated, on the browned paper. I DO question the statement that it "is a simple affair to prepare", and wonder about including the 'shells' of five eggs:

"Should be made at any rate the day before it is required. It is a simple affair to prepare it. Procure a couple of feet and put them on the fire in three quarts of water; let them boil for five hours, during which keep skimming. Pass the liquor through a hair sieve into a basin, and let it firm, after which remove all the oil and fat. Next take a teacupful of

water, two wineglassfuls of sherry, the juice of
half a dozen lemons and the rind of one, the
whites and shells of five eggs, half a pound of
fine white sugar, and whisk the whole till the
sugar be melted, then add the jelly, place the
whole on the fire in an enameled stewpan, and
keep actively stirring till the composition comes
to the boil. Pass it all through a jelly-bag, and
then place in the molds."

HICKORY BARK SYRUP

Patsy Morgan, Scottsville, KY
via her Grandmother, Lottie Conner

Wash bark from a Shagbark Hickory Tree.
Boil bark in water until the water is the color
of coffee. In a large kettle over slow heat mix 4
lb. white sugar, 4 lb. brown sugar and enough
bark water to flavor to taste (about one cup).
Heat to boiling—but don't boil; just enough to
melt the sugar. Put into jars to enjoy for a
country breakfast treat. (Patsy's mother made
this delicacy; so has she.)

Shave And A Hair Cut: Two Bits

Classy hair salons in the Big Apple nowadays, I hear tell, often whack over a hundred bucks out of a'body's budget for a single styling, shampoo, set, and the tip. That applies for grooming the locks of either men or women. A far cry from the two bits or less my Daddy and brother Bill paid in the 30s-40s for a personalized cut. And from the freebies I got at my Aunt Bert's hand in the days when a penny meant something.

The Sabbath, when I was a child, was Holy. Ironing a dress, hoeing a row of grassy corn, sewing a ripped seam, or mopping a dirty floor was absolutely unheard of on Sunday. Yet many menfolk, like my Daddy and brother, often walked two, three miles on Sunday mornings to a hair-cutting-neighbor's house. Got their hair cut, got a "trim" as my Daddy called it, and they still made it to church via mule and wagon for 11 o'clock preaching.

Such Sabbath-hair-cutting wasn't considered a sin, even in our conservative neck of the woods; after the accommodating neighbor busted out corn middles with a shovel and hill sweep six days a week that 'uz his only available time. It wasn't like he was piling up 'filthy lucre' in a fancy salon, though; sometimes he was paid a dime, maybe occasionally given a quarter, but more often the penniless folks just said, "I'm much obliged t'ye, 'til ye're better paid, Jake." And the good neighbor'd reply, "That's OK, Ira, glad t'accommodate ye."

Hair cutting was done out on the porch, weather permitting, back then. The barber chair for men was a nail keg; to elevate small boys they sometimes placed a child's rocker in the seat of a straight chair and hoisted the little one therein. A guano sack or an old sheet was wrapped around the individual's neck

before the procedure began; the same wrap
was shaken of its hair and used many times
before being laundered.

Tools for home barbering were simple
also. A slender pair of scissors, a comb—which
was also used repeatedly on many heads before being washed, a pair of hand-operated
clippers, and a straight razor. Occasionally,
the cutter might also have a cake of shaving
soap in a cup with a little round brush for
lathering up a customer's neck.

The home-barbers with which my family
was most acquainted were not professionals;
had been off for no barbering courses. They
learned while doing and the ten-cent haircuts
often spoke of that truth. As my older brother
grew into his teenage years he'd grumble about
his hair being botched, or gapped, or looking
like "a bowl was turned upside down over my
head and he jest clipped around it." As Elvis
began to wear his hair long with sideburns it
tore my brother up to have a barber, as he said,
"just skin me." Of course those crew cuts—
which came close to a shaved head—suited my
Daddy just fine for his boys; that way he didn't
have to come up with the dimes as often, nor
the money for Wild Root Creame Oil to slick the

long hair back.

But the thing my brothers complained about most, and sometimes little Doug cried about, was the "all-fired pulling." The pulling that seemed to just go-along-with those clippers which worked only as the barber pumped his hand back and forth, open and closed, on their handles. The terrible pulling that resulted if the clippers were very cheap and very dull. And the awful pain that ensued when the barber finished up the cut by having the victim bend his head over for a dry neck shave using a dull straight razor, dry because he wouldn't take the time and effort to lather up with the soap. "Jest like pulling hairs out by th' roots," my brother Bill would come home whining.

Many old timers like my octogenarian friend, Mr. Albert Lee, remember those unpleasant hair cuts. Mr. Lee recalls, " I got many-a-them-ten-cent-hair-pullin'-cuts from Ervin Thrasher, you know, he 'uz a preacher and he also cut hair."

Continuing, Mr. Lee shares, "You know, they 'uz these two fellers, two barbers in town, back in the 30s. Jim Jones, well, he only charged twenty-five cents fer a cut but Sam, he charged thirty-five; said he couldn't make it fer less, what with his modern pedal-driven, adjustable barber chair and the red-and-white 'candy' pole outside. Well, once a feller had bought some jacks and brought 'em to the livery stable down close to Sam's place. And the jacks commenced t'braying one Saturday morning, just wouldn't shut up. Well, Sadie wuz in town and ye know, there in front uv Sam she said, "Listen...listen, ain't that jacks a-braying?" Sam, the competitor, spoke up right quick and answered her, "Naw, that ain't jacks, that's coming from Jim Jones' barber shop, he's over there a-giving somebody one uv them dry shaves."

My Uncle Ferman shared his hair cut memories with me and my younger sister Betty in 1991, as he passed his 85th birthday, memories of him and our Daddy, Ira. "Yea, hair cuts 'uz thirty-five cents at Gordo. But Mr. Homer McAteer cut at home fer fifteen cents." Betty, flabbergasted over the price, registered her surprise by sliding in her,"SHUT-YOUR-MOUTH! YOU DON'T SAY!" Meanwhile Uncle Ferman never slowed down, "Yea, me 'n Ira'd go down there a lot uv times on Sunday but you'd have to wait a long time. But I allez give him fifty cents fer cutting two heads. But it 'uz thirty-five-cents a long time; Roy Johnson and Preacher (Grover) Pate he cut mine a long time for thirty-five cents. Got a better cut than you do now for $5.00. They charge me $5.00; course I don't go very often; trim my own a little with a razor from time 't time, me 'er Gertrude one."

Males aren't the only ones who have endured suffering down through the years in the quest for crowning glory upon their heads. My mama's childhood saw girls like Zelda who suffered mental anguish because they were forbidden by their fathers to cut their hair; others were subjected to boyish bobs, Dutch boy bobs—where the hair was cut straight across and the bangs were cut straight also. Other maidens nearly pulled their brains out while ratting their hair, trying to make it appear bigger, more bouffant. Zelda confides that she suffered terrible headaches for years and still attributes them to the weight of her long red tresses, hair down past her waist, which her Daddy wouldn't allow cut from the day she was born. However, on the very day she turned twenty-one, became a woman of her own, she hurried to the beauty parlor and had it most all clipped off.

I was blessed with wavy hair for several years—thin, but nontheless wavy. I received very little hair treatment back then, that is— not counting the horrible 'styling' my older sister Frances inflicted upon me when we were both wee tots. My usual hair beautification, though, was a twice-a-year cut when Aunt Bert came to visit on Sunday afternoons. Plus an occasional rolling with curlers made by cutting Prince Albert Tobacco cans into strips and covering the strips with pieces of brown paper poke. Or once-in-a-blue-moon when Grandma Shirley rolled my hair in rags and then let it twirl down the next day in long, graceful Shirley Temple curls.

But at the age of thirteen my auntie decided to spruce me up with a new-fangled Toni Home Permanent. After a 'few hours' of torture with the tight curlers and the stinking lotion, however, I emerged—not beautiful, as expected. BUT FRIZZED, FRIZZED, FRIZZED!! Ruined for life, I thought at the time.

I was fortunate, however, that my torment and pain in acquiring the overly-tight curls did not compare with that of my city cousin, Elizabeth. At that time she was going ever so often to the beauty parlor to get her hair 'fried,' to get a permanent wave, as they called it. She told me that they rolled her hair around little metal rods. Then, using a little tool, they tightened each one of the rods tighter than Dick's hat band. Next they hooked her up to a big old machine, put a metal clamp over each of the rolls on her head, and turned the gizmo on. As the hair was being curled she said it sizzled, sort of like bacon frying, and it puffed out smoke. But when everything was unhooked and the rolls were unwound—talk about curls! Did Elizabeth EVER have curls to last!

Hair styles come and hair styles go, or so they have the six decades I've been on this earth. During that time the cost of haircuts have gone from a thin dime to hundreds of dollars, have made the circuit from the gapped 'personalized cuts' my brother Bill received all the way to the modern personalized cuts, those which are now sculptured with each person's individual's design. The cuts have been ratted, poufed, and teased. They were once enhanced by Wild Root and Brilliantine; now they are adorned with mousse, jels, sprints, etc. But I'd be willing to wager, and me not even a betting gal, that you'd be hard-pressed today to find

someone who'd cut your hair in a more neighborly way than my Aunt Bert did long ago for
free or than Mr. Ervin did back then for just a
thin dime or no more than two bits.

If times get worse...

There's Always Possum 'N Taters

I read with interest of a recent Wild Meat Feast. Meat delicacies were served to hundreds at the event. There was buffalo, armadillo, moose, deer, beaver, elk, turkey, rabbit, squirrel, and the Great Depression standby, opossum. The present state of the economy made me wonder about the shindig. Wonder if, instead of a nostalgic remembrance, the gathering was really a sharpening up of palates for the future.

I reckon that during the hard times of the 30s our huge family reacted like one of the recent feast participants who said, "We'll eat anything that won't eat us first." Never knew of our neighbors nor us being reduced to cooking pole cats, but we did often enjoy racoon, better know as coon, and opossum meat, or 'possum as we called it.

Having a possum in a pan meant more than meat for supper when I was growing up. The animal's soft grey hide, when sold to the tanner for three to five dollars, translated into money for shoes or coffee or flour. It was a better return on Daddy's time to hunt possums on a frosty moonlit night in October, November than working at the sawmill come daylight. Yep, he could put more food on his table and shoe leather on his younguns' cold feet by moseying over to the persimmon trees with the old hound dog than by public works.

Daddy knew the location of every 'simmon tree in our county, I reckon. Knew that as soon as the first frost came and sweetened the orange fruit, the possums were gonna climb those trees and stuff themselves nightly; (possums weren't fools, they knew they had to rush to beat human beings to the delicious soft fruit.)

So Daddy'd take my brother Bill and they'd head out on a nippy night. It wouldn't be long before Old Drum would start baying up a 'simmon tree; have him a possum treed.

Shotgun shells were such a rare commodity during the Depression and WW II days until Daddy dared not waste a shell on an animal "grinnin' like a possum" from the top of a simmon tree. Once in a blue moon a startled possum could, by folks shaking a tree vigorously, be hurled to the ground. More often, however, it was like the old saying,"This is a dry drought and holds on like a possum on a limb." At those times Bill might go clamoring up the tree to gently dislodge the animal. However, an entire tree was at times sacrificed to get the animal, chopped down with an ax brought along on the hunt for that very purpose.

Daddy always endeavored to bring the possums home in one healthy piece; often the captured animal was better off than the hunters who had walked ten, fifteen miles through briar patches and what-have-ye all night long. Come daylight the creature would be checked out. If it was a skinny thing it went into a pen to be fed and fattened before slaughtering. Some folks even fattened them up on sweet potatoes, perhaps as a prelude to the final feast of possum 'n 'taters.

My Mama now, at age 87, admits to having been the one who had to kill many 'a possum, once they were fattened. " Did it by laying a board across one's neck, then pulling upwards with it's hind feet, breaking it's neck swiftly," she explains.

Once dead the possums at our house were skinned. Starting from the hind legs in much the same manner in which a squirrel was skinned, the skin was zipped up over the head. Then the head was cut off and discarded. The skin was next stretched over a board, meaty side out, to dry and be sold.

Some families, however, who did not wish to tan the hide, removed the possum's hair like they did when slaughtering a hog. My friend Grace Barrett from South Carolina and her brother Charles recently detailed for me the manner in which their folks cleaned a possum with ashes.

"Heat water in a black wash pot. Dip your hand in two, three times to make sure the water is hot, but not too hot. Gradually stir into the water some ashes from well-burned oak wood. Then be very cautious that the ash water, with it's lye content, does not get onto your skin. Tie a strong string around the possum's head for holding onto. While holding the possum's tail and the string, dip the 'possum in and out of the lye water, checking occasionally until the hair begins to turn loose. Then lay the possum on a board and, using a dull knife, scrape all it's hair off. "The possum's skin will be as white as a baby's behind," Charles says.

My Mama would say that the next step to a delicious meal is to discard the animal's head and insides, wash the remaining meat thoroughly, and parboil in a large pot with salted water until it is tender; some added a pod of hot, red pepper to the boiling water. Then remove the meat to a baking pan. Place partially cooked, peeled and quartered, sweet potatoes around the meat. Bake in a moderately hot oven (two sticks of stovewood) until it is beginning to brown. Serve piping hot with a pot of turnip greens, pot likker, and corn bread for the feast of your life.

Bro. Benny, however, said that when he enjoyed a possum for his Christmas dinner in 1991 he skipped the parboiling. After killing and cleaning the animal captured from the 'simmon tree near his back door, he just put the lean feller into a baking pan and sprinkled it with salt. To baste it better he laid some fat meat slices over the possum and put uncooked sweet 'taters around it. He baked it in the oven for an hour or so, then sprinkled brown sugar over the entire dish and continued baking until tender. His recipe after that: "Hope everyone will leave so you can eat it all by yourself!"

It does look like America might be heading for hard times once more. But the news is not all bad. I read in my Farm Bureau newspapers that folks are planting 'simmon trees right and left—mostly to feed more possums with, I reckon (since most modern folks wouldn't know that a green 'simmon will pucker their mouth up for a couple o' hours, at least.) And most nights when I'm out driving near my home in the boondocks " I jest never seed the lack 'o possums lumbering alongside folks' yards and cow trails." So even if we have another depression I figure there's gonna be plenty of good eating for folks— always having possum and 'taters. Just one word of caution, however: send for my Mama to break those possums' necks for you. Don't do like the feller I read about last week.

Seems the man's possum ran into the

kitchen. He grabbed his shotgun, and once the creature ran to the tater bin and "played possum", the man fired. Hit a gas main and blew up the house. Missed the possum but did find it's charred remains beside the baked taters in the debris of the house. That's so like the goodness that surrounds our lives: Even when misfortune overtakes us, it seems the Good Lord always provides our possum 'n taters.

Ring! Ring! Ring That Dinner Bell!

Tell Saint Peter at the Golden Gate,

That he's jest gonna hafta wait

'Cause I hear Mama once more

ringin' that dinner bell!

During the Great Depression Mama wasted nothing. When stewing a chicken to make broth for dumplings or dressing or chicken pie she used even the head and the feet, throwing away only the feathers, the insides, and the toenails. And the dishes made from it was delicious. Stew up some chicken and try the following dumpling recipe:

OLD FASHIONED DUMPLINGS
Nona Tindall, St. Cloud, GA

2 C flour   1 tsp sugar

3 eggs (if it's self-rising, add 4 eggs)

Mix dough well. Turn onto floured board and knead as for biscuits. Roll out and cut in strips. Add to lightly boiling chicken broth for dumplings. Add meat of chicken, heat, serve. (Nona sometimes uses a modern touch: Adds Lipton Onion Soup Mix to the dumpling mixture for a great taste in chicken broth.)

HAM AND EGG PIE
Elizabeth Akeridge, Coker, AL

2 C diced ham	*3 hard boiled eggs*
6 C water	*2 T butter or oleo*
Dumplings	*Pastry for crust*

Cut bits of ham from a ham bone. Place water and ham in a sauce pan and bring to a boil. Turn heat down and simmer 20 min. Add pepper (salt if needed) to taste and stir in 2 T butter or oleo.

Bring to a boil and add dumplings and sliced eggs. Pour into a casserole dish and put crust on top. Bake in a 400 degree oven until browned on top.

Dumplings for Ham Pie

1 1/3 C Plain flour	*1/4 tsp salt*
2 T oil	

Enough cold water to make a dough you

can roll. Mix all together and roll out real thin.
Cut into strips and then into 1 1/2-2 inch
pieces. Drop into the above mixture.

Ham Pie Crust Pastry

1 1/2 C Plain flour   *1/4 tsp salt*

1/2 C lard (shortening)   *3-4 tsp cold water*

Cut in shortening until it resembles coarse
cornmeal. Stir in cold water to just hold together. Roll out for pie crust. Completely cover
the pie with the crust.

"I, Faye Brown, have eaten Elizabeth's
Ham Pie; I can testify that it's 'Yum, Yum, good
eatin'; just like Mama's."

DOUGH BOY
(Meal Soup)
Zelda Lawrence, Coker, AL

Boil 3-4 ham hocks with plenty of water
until thoroughly cooked. Remove the bones.
Mix 1/2 cup of self-rising meal with enough
water to make a smooth paste. Bring the broth
to a full boil. Add the meal mixture to the
broth, stirring rapidly to prevent lumping.
Turn the heat down to low and simmer for a few
minutes.

This is a delicious soup for cold winter
days, or great when one is sick!

CUSH

Ruby Perritt, St. George, GA

Ruby's father was taught this Indian recipe by Billy Bowlegs, a Seminole Indian, near Moore Haven, FL many years ago.

Slice and fry white meat, cool. Break meat into small pieces. Add to corn meal in an ovenware container. Mix enough water to make a sort of paste, and add chopped onions. Cook the mixture in the oven (of a wood-burning cookstove, preferably) until the onion is done. It should be the consistency of stuffing, and be moist, not dry.

"OH, TO HAVE A 'BAIT' OF MACARONI AND CHEESE"

The following Macaroni and Cheese dish is a 'meat,' a main dish, not a vegetable as it's considered on many menus today. When we were growing up it was a rare treat, indeed, for Daddy to bring home a slab of Hoop Cheese from the Mercantile in town. We kids would fain have eaten it all immediately, as most would ice cream or chocolate drops, but Mama insisted on hoarding the biggest part of it for making the main course at Sunday Dinner, Macaroni and Cheese. I remember my brother

Bill saying that one thing he was "gonna do when I grow up, have all the cheese I want, just have me a big bait of it." (And, I believe Bill's been able to realize his big dream of 'having all the cheese to eat that his heart desired'—or at least he did before they started counting cholesterol.)

It is hard to say which pulled me most toward marrying into the BROWN FAMILY back in 1956—whether my great love for Joe or love for the Macaroni and Cheese Bake which his mother, Elizabeth (Doodley) Brown made very often. Following is a recipe very similar to her and my mother's wonderful concoction:

MARVELOUS MACARONI AND CHEESE
Ovelia Hatter, Brookwood, AL

2 C uncooked macaroni	1 tsp salt
1 1/4 C (chopped) cheese	6 C water
1/2 tsp salt	2 eggs
2 T margarine	3 C milk

Bring water and 1/2 tsp salt to a boil. Add macaroni, stirring. Cook until done, drain. Put cooked macaroni into a bowl. Add 1 tsp salt and mix. Add cheese and oleo. Grease a medium size baking dish. Pour mixture into dish. Beat 2 eggs with fork, thoroughly. Add 3 C milk and stir. Pour mixture over macaroni. Bake in 350 degree oven for 40 minutes. Serve piping hot!

THE WORLD'S FIRST JIGGLERS (JELLO)

Nita Nettles, Alachua, FL

"It was a cold, December day. My parents had helped a neighbor kill hogs. Among other meat my mother was given four pigs feet. She cleaned and cooked them tender, preparing to make Pickled Pigs Feet. Then she took the water where the feet had been cooked, skimmed all excess fat from it, added a little sugar and Watkins lemon extract. Then she put it in a bowl and placed it out on the roof of the back porch overnight, for refrigeration. The next day my sister and I were treated to what is now known as Jigglers or Jello, " thus shares Nita.

SAVING LOTS FOR LATER

So sorry space is forcing me to wait until Book number five to share with you my Mama's wonderful chicken 'n dressing, her squirrel stew, fried squirrel and rabbit, turtle meat, and salmon croquettes recipes plus my Granny Porter's and Sister Betty's famous Brunswick Stew.

I have also had to save for a subsequent book numerous wonderful recipes contributed by many of you folks. Recipes for things which "fancy up a meal:" pickles from peaches, cucumbers, and cabbage, tomato catsup, corn relish, chow chow, spiced tomatoes, and pepper sauce. Also pear honey, and preserves from pears, figs, and watermelon rinds.

When The Preacher's Wife
Got Salted Down

(or Pounding The Preacher)

A music minister and his new wife, both still wet behind the ears and students, were recently employed by our church. Sensing they were "up agin it" and also wishing to extend a royal welcome, the body of believers decided to give them an old-time pounding. The younguns were flabbergasted—appreciative of the food, all right—but downright flabbergasted with vittles to overflow their pantry, never having heard of the church custom.

Pounding the preacher was a common

ritual in the evangelical churches of the South during the Great Depression. It was, most often, a way of expressing welcome into the new church community at the beginning of a minister's term. However, if the Servant of the Lord stayed on the same field two or three or more years, he might be given a pounding every year.

During the very lean years when churches were able to pay their leaders very little cash, "the pounding" grew in significance. Sometimes the ritual "Spel't out if'n there'uz meal in the barrel 'r not," one old-timer filled me in, referring to the Biblical incident during the severe drought and famine in Israel when, because of the prophet Elijah, the widow's barrel miraculously never became empty of meal for bread. "Yessirree, God A'Mighty working through us to p'vide meal in the barrel 'n oil in the cruse," the feller had continued explaining to me.

Getting right down to the truth of the matter, the poundings given by church members often supplied ALL, or the major part of the food a minister and his wife had to eat. A pile of food stuffs DID COME IN on those occasions when the church leaders put out the word, "We're gonna surprise the preacher with a pounding. Just bring what'eer ye can spare wi' ye t' Prayer Meeting next Wednesday night."

AND BRING IT the good country folk did! They'd roll in with their wagons piled high, especially if it was the fall of the year after they'd harvested. There'd be turns o' meal, fresh ginned. Some ginned half-and-half, for meal and grits. And baskets of sweet 'taters, just dug. Jars and jars of canned goods which the ladies had labored over during the hot summers. And you'd have thought they were taking the string beans, tomatoes, vegetable soup mix, pickled peaches, blackberry jam, and peach marmalade to the County Fair the way they sacrificed their prettiest and best "fer the Rev'r'nd."

Some would come with dried apples, sealed up in jars also—to keep out the insects. And if the new preacher had a young, city-bred wife they'd tuck in a recipe for making fried apple pies. (And afterwards they'd offer to come over and teach her if she'd like. Properly, she'd always say, "Of course, of course, that would be Sooooo nice of you," whether she meant it or not.) And alongside the apples there'd be a jar of hot pepper sauce, with some one chuckling, behind the crowd "...causing the preacher's s' easy going — this'll steam 'em up sometimes, I betcha." Meanwhile the preacher's family just oooohhh'd and aaaahhhhh'd and blessed "you good folks," and thank'd and praised the Lord, no end.

Ministers of the Word—all in their eighties, nineties—with whom I spoke recently, remembered fondly The Poundings they received long ago. Rev. Albert Elzie Lee laughingly told of preparing to go to his first pastorate. Said his father, making his hand into a fist and punching it back and forth, hitting the air, had laughed and said, "Those church folks'll pound you, son; they'll pound you all right." "But," Mr. Lee added, "they did give me and my wife lots of things. One lady even gave us a cow, said she owed The Lord $40 on her tithe and didn't have the money—it being The Depression—and since someone had offered her $40 for the cow—she wanted "to even up with The Lord by pounding me with the cow."

Another minister who had also told of receiving a cow at a pounding explained, "One feller came to church the night of the pounding with the old jersey tied behind his wagon. Then another, the neighbor he was in cahoots with, came d'rectly behind him, bringing 50 bales of sweet alfalfa hay for her winter feed. She wadn't much to look at but she could sure fill a milk bucket."

One Man of the Cloth told of receiving a milk goat from a parishioner. "Of course," Bro. Jim said, "he didn't bring the goat to the church. But on the night of the pounding he announced his gift and then walked her over the next morning." Mr. Jim then filled in the rest of the story, "Times wuz s'hard I'uz proud to get the goat for milk for our younguns. She'd dropped a kid not more'n four months b'fore and she'd give lots o' milk. But we had a time milking 'er fer awhile, her being us'ta Miz Allie a'milkin' er and us never milked a goat b'fore. Why, she'd cut a rusty ever time my wife er I come into the lot. And when we started pullin' on 'er, trying to git her milk to come down, she'd really cut loose, commence to kicking and jumping and switching that tail. Now, don't get me wrong, I sure 'preciated the milk but many-a-time when we's out there wrestlin' with that fetched goat, if we could've had our druthers, we'd a took a little cash instead."

Bro. Ray and Jeannette said someone once pounded them with a little pig. "We lived

in a country parsonage so we built him a pen,
raised him, and slaughtered him. Was proud
to get the meat," they said. They remembered
also, having farmers in their congregation who
would, during the winter, kill two hogs at a
time. One for themselves and one for the
preacher. "They just pounded us all year round,
not on just one week," Bro. Ray recalled happily.

Yep, several preachers agreed, some years
they'd received a wide variety of dried, canned,
or fresh meat, fruit, and vegetables at the
poundings. "Then other years,"—they shook
their heads— "it was unbelievable how you'd
get so much of the same thing. Fifty jars of
beets, five bushels of dried peas, or twenty
huge pumpkins. And the kids not even liking
beets or dried peas or pumpkin—but they had
to eat it, sure did."

The young minister and his wife who
were recently pounded at our church were
fortunate. They received a whole passel of
stuff, all kinds, a good dukesmixture; things
modern young folks eat—from Fritos and Pepsis
to Nachos and Cokes to Gift Certificates for
free meals at McDonalds and Red Lobster, "for
the seafood lover in them". It was obvious they

were thrilled to pieces.

Miss Paralee, age 96 and holding, who lives over there at Scratch Gravel—which is a little piece down the road from Frog Ridge—told me about a different pounding. One which, I think—excuse the pun—takes the cake. She said, "It happened years and years ago, way out in the country at a little church called the HALLELUJAH, HE'S A'COMING CHURCH. Had them a new preacher called, heard he had a wife and nine kids to feed. So they put out the word for everybody "to bring a Pound" for them on such and such a night. Well, the church wuz packed, full as a tick —and the preacher uz bound to uv knowed sumptin was going on the way everybody was whispering 'round about where to leave the stuff, or saying they had left their's out in the wagon. And you could even see some folks a-branging in bulging toe sacks and guano sacks and a-struggling to slide 'em under the benches.

"Well, after the sanging and the testimonies—where Miss Beulah praised God fer sending the folks to pull her jersey cow outta that old abandoned well the week before—well, the preacher got up to preach. And he wadn't more'n five minutes into his sermon 'till you

could feel those hell fires a'scorching the town
drunks and the harlots—and, right off the bat,
Lullabell—who'd had her husband strayed
away by a harlot years before —well, Lullabelle
leaned over to me and whispered, 'Laws-a-
mercy, honey, he's so good I wish't t'th'Lord I'd
a'put a jar uv my famous fig preserves in my
sack fer 'im.'

"Well, the preacher preached his heart
out — now I don't just recollect if anybody went
to the mourner's bench afterwards er not—but
I know they's a pile uv em there that should've
gone. But when it was time for the
bennydiction—well—the chairman of the
pounding committee, Junior Lee, I b'lieve it
twas. Well, he stood up and said he wanted to
say a word. So atter he'd rattled on and on
about the virtues —as he'd been told em—the
virtues of the new preacher. Well, he finally
upped and said we had brung him a pounding!
And of course the preacher and his whole
family 'tended surprised to death.

"Then Junior Lee said would everybody
just brang their pounds up to the front, com-
mencing on the right front side of the church.
Just brang it up and hold each thang up for the
folks to see. And to then hand it on to the

preacher and his family as they stood there at the front, accepting it and a-laying it down on the front benches.

"Folks went scuddlin' outside to brang theirs in—those what didn't have em under their benches already. And then it all began! Lord, Lord, it all commenced. Now, don't git me wrong, chile, they wuz a powerful lotta good stuff had been brung. But it weren't long fore it began to be shameful to the core.

"You see, first went Hattie Bell, and—among other thangs—she held up a five-pound-sack of salt and handed it to the preacher's wife. When Pearl came up with her husband, Jessie, she also presented a five-pound-sack of salt. Then it was Hortense and Junior Lee's turn, another bag of salt. Vergil and Mollie had salt; as did Gertrude and Lozell. On and on it went, like-you'd-not-a-believed if I, Paralee Hawthorne, wadn't a'sitting here this minute a'telling it with my snaggle-tooth-mouth."

Hardly pausing for a breath, Paralee went on, "I ain't never seen sich a sight uv salt since God eber made me, ain't neber seen the beat uv it, ever' which way ye looked—jest salt, salt, and more salt. Think't th' last counting uv it—not out loud, of course, but some uv em figured it in their heads, under their breaths, mind ye,and made a good note uv it. They'uz thirteen uv them little five-pound-sacks of salt brung that one night fer the preacher's wife.

"Now I ain't one to tote tales," Paralee defended herself to me, explaining, "and ye can annie-lyze it backards 'n forards til the cows come home, but I say t'weren't no co-in-ci-dence! Some of the saints tried to hush it up, said not to make no big-to-do over it. 'Lowed everbody was jest a'thanking ahead to hog-killing time, thanking the preacher'd need to kill and salt down a passel o'shoats to feed his brood.

"But Sarienell Poindexter, I think, had as good an explanashun of it as you'd find. Sarienell said it was like a prophecy from God. And she figured it all had a meaning. Said the preacher had ways like Lot in the Bible, what with his departing from his former location and a-choosing the rich part of the land there where the HALLELUJAH, HE'S A COMING CHURCH was located.

"And, it figured— she said— that the Reverend's wife represented Lot's wife. And fer the members to buy out every sack of salt that the rolling store feller and the local Yellow

Front Store had on hand—to buy every last one
o' them and present 'em to the preacher's
helpmeet—without any fore-planning or con-
niving—well, it sure looked like it spelled out
doom for the preacher and his woman, like
their sins had maybe caught up with 'em, like
Lot's wife's did —with her being turned to salt
by the Almighty, turned to salt for her hidden,
sinful ways."

    "Like I said," concluded Paralee, "I ain't
one to go spreadin' gossip. But it shore seemed
like that perticuler Pounding Fer The Preacher
turned out to be a sign from God, more'n it was
food fer the hungry. Least wise, I heard tell
that when the preacher's wife got wind of
Sarienell's theorie—well, it'uz the next year,
after they'd moved on to another field of labor—but I heard tell she got all broke up over
it when she heard the Sarienell inter-per-ta-
shun. And I heard it from a r'liabl' source that
it finally run her crazy as a bessie bug.

    " So, chile, you'uns can go and pound yo
young minister iffen ye want," Paralee advised
as I took my leave of her recently, " but I jest
know that I've been mighty leary uv them
poundings ever since the HALLELUJAH
preacher's wife got herself all salted down."

Lightnin' Rods 'N 'Lectric Pow'r

(or Keep Those Jiggers Outta My Corn Pone)

Two of the greatest puzzles of my young life were lightnin' (lightning) rods and 'lectric pow'r (electricity); they always kept burning questions in my mind. I had read in my schoolbooks about Benjamin Franklin discovering 'lectric'ty by holding a kite with a door key attached during a bad thunderstorm. And my teachers had informed me of Thomas Edison's invention of the light bulb; of his discoveries which had led to many luxuries.

The revelations, I thought, had translated into " man's ability to grab the lightning out of the sky" and let it make the big-fan-with-paddles in the top of the City Drug Store

go round-and-round, cooling folks who came
to town on Saturdays. Had been the means by
which a light shone brightly in the top of my
schoolroom without the teacher lighting a kerosene lamp like we did at home. Even provided
for my girlfriend's family to scrub their clothes
in an automatic Bendix washer which was
bolted to the kitchen floor, to clean the garments without a rub board and black iron pot
like my family used down at the spring. Pure
Magic!

Having seen and heard all my life of the
devastation wrought by lightning increased
my wonder over man's ability "to capture" the
deadly force. Bill and I had been the ones who
found Daisy, our milk cow; found her fried
body underneath the splintered lone oak tree
following the frightening fireworks of a hot
summer's thunderstorm.

And our family had grieved with the
neighbors when lightning struck their barn
one fall night. We heard the loud POP and from
our windows saw the 40-ft-flames(the flash of
light like I always figured it'd be when Jesus
splits the eastern sky, coming to earth again).
God's 'lectric'ty struck and— in a matter of
seconds, it seemed— ate up the loft filled with

fresh hay and the stalls with cows and yearlin's;
left them all cremated, just a pile of glowing
ashes where the folks' worldly treasures and
their dreams had been. It was no wonder that
after that when Daddy had us in the storm pit,
he'd say, "Listen, listen—LORDY, LORDY, I
b'lieve lighnin's hit the barn!"

But the answer to all this tragedy long
ago, my siblings and I knew, lay—in part—
with obeying our Daddy's instructions about
what to do and what not to do when it was
lightning. We knew that dogs drew lightning so
no matter how much we loved an old hound it
could not be allowed on the porch when a
thunderstorm came up.

In fact we had to go inside the house
ourselves, regardless of the steamy weather.
We could not sit on an iron bedstead, nor near
the fireplace, which—like open doors and windows—were an invitation for lightning to strike.
Nor could we cook on the iron cookstove nor
use smoothing irons. Using the sewing machine, scissors, or a needle and thimble was
also out of the question.

Lightnin' rods on the tops of one's house
and barn held the key to safety, I felt long-ago.
Perhaps even more so than your Daddy's do's

and don'ts. But the devices, with all of their exquisite beauty and their afforded protection, were just a pie-in-the-sky dream for us.

Whenever Frances and I accompanied Daddy to the gristmill—our feet dangling from the wagon's rear end— or when we walked the miles to the New Church to attend Singing School, we passed Dr. Shackelford's huge gabled house with it's lightning rods pointing to the sky. The rods were attached to the top of the tall structure, with their round glass balls like little suns, struck through with arrows , heading heavenward. Others had adorned arrows intersecting the vertical rods, directing the lightnin' to the East, to the West. They looked so authoritative, like the good country doctor had looked when he stood over me once, pronouncing that I had the "neumonia." I just knew that lightnin' would never defy those fancy, stalwart instruments and hit the doctor's house —but our tenant farming one? We just had to take our chanches with the temper fits of Miss Nature; I figured that at any moment our number would come up and we'd be dust-to-dust, just like the preacher said everybody'd be eventually.

Yet for all it's destructive potential, the

power from lightnin' had it's good points,
leastwise that's what folks hear from the
Wiggins' family down in Moundville, AL. Seems
Mr. John was cured of a terrible arthritic
condition when lightnin' killed his plowing
partner and their two mules and sent its volt-
age through his own cripped body (as he briefly
held a plow handle during a monstrous thunderstorm).

Taking the good and the bad into consid-
eration and deciding for/against the installa-
tion of 'tamed lightnin' (electric power) in our
house wasn't my decision when the pow'r
com'ny (power company) started putting up
lines in our neck uv the woods. Part of me
feared it, just like the old woman up there on
Pea Ridge did. She (the one who had 26 cats
and who still plowed with the oxen) was dead-
set against the innovation. "Figure", she said,
"it'll be jest like lightnin' what's not harnessed,
kill 'a'body more apt than not."

Another side of me was as excited as
Mama. Thrilled to pieces to get those light
bulbs dangling from the ceiling. And the 'lectric
airn (iron) so we didn't have to worry about
ashes and soot from the flat airns getting onto
Daddy's white shirts. And the frigidaire (a

generic term for refrigerator) was the best part of all. It meant we could drink iced tea for lunch and cold milk for supper. Could convert the little strawberries from our spring garden and Old Bossy's milk into ice cream to refresh ourselves when we came, hot and tired, from the Back Forty.

Of course, the coming of electricity to our house also meant that Daddy spent a lot of time out by the fuse box, watching it, reporting, "It's jest a-whizzin' round 'n round;" and a-worryin' about the "three-dollar-a-month - light-bill."

My childhood puzzlement with lightnin', lightnin' rods, and 'lectric'ty has continued down through the years. My husband and children have derided as I have viewed new appliances with skepticism: "That electric hairdryer is probably gonna make me go bald-headed." "I just don't know about sleeping under an electric blanket. What-if I drank too much Coke, had an accident, and woke up wet and electrocuted." And, "I'm not sold on those microwave ovens. I jest figure they're gonna put some 'jiggers' in my food and kill me."

Yep, most of my life I've been afraid of the unharnassed 'lectric'ty, of lightnin', cause I've never had the protective rods atop my house. But now my weatherman has eased my mind; his National Lightning Detection Network helps me locate lightning strikes and overcome my fears.

Yet at the same time comes puzzling news about the harnessed 'lectrical pow'r; (always at least One of 'Em fueling the flames in my mind). Studies are now proving that electro-magnetic fields are very dangerous. That a body is more likely to get leukemia who shaves with an electric razor, who plays video games, who is awakened by an electric clock, or who sleeps under an electric blanket (and just when I got a new, queen-sized one for Christmas), or one who cooks their food in a microwave oven. It's probably gonna turn out just like me and the old woman plowing her oxen up on Pea Ridge half-a-century-ago figured. Like she told the pow'r com'ny back then, "Naw, siree, mister, ye ain't puttin' no pow'r poles on my place. 'A'body's lib'ls't t'eat enuf uv that 'lectricity in their cornpone alone to kill 'em."

Mama Had A Thing For Tender Veggies

(And so did a lot of other country women long ago.)

My newspaper ran a column recently urging folks, for their health's sake, to occasionally observe 'Veggie Night'—that is, for one meal to abstain from meat and eat vegetables only. I'm all for it!

To be perfectly honest with you, as children we repeatedly experienced 'Veggie Night.'

In fact, our family had entire vegetable months with only one, two messes of young fryers thrown in, whenever the preachers came to visit. But even when our table fare of veggies stretched endlessly during spring and summer months you didn't hear us begging God to miraculously send up quail into our camp. That's because our Mama knew how to grow, cook, and serve vegetables like you seldom encounter today; she had a thing for young, tender veggies, if you will. Try the following recipes—either Mama's or a spinoff—and you'll agree.

MAMA'S ENGLISH PEAS
AND GRAB'LED 'TATERS

Go out to the garden and pick all the English peas off the vines; get them while they are still very tender, long before the pods are completely "filled out" and beginning to turn yellow. Might as well go ahead and pull up the pea vines and take them to the shade, sit down and pull the peas off, and then throw the vines over the fence to Old Bossy. Because it is a tried and tested fact: you'll only get two messes of English peas from a planting. One for the family and a mess of vines for the cow.

To complete the heavenly gourmet dish of English peas each spring Mama would add miniature red potatoes, no bigger than a man's thumb. Now, she had a ritual for grab'l'ng (graveling) small irish potatoes. As the plants began to get a little size on them she watched for a small crack to appear in the soil near the plant's roots. Then, equipping herself with a fork and an old boiler—one that was leaking regardless of all the mend-its in it—she went forth into the 'tater patch. While gently bending a green plant sideways Mama scratched soil from underneath, exposing the potato's roots with their varied-sized potatoes—from tiny nodules, to pea size, and upward to walnuts. After carefully stealing a couple of the largest ones—the hikker nuts—she firmly replaced the soil and proceeded to the next plant for another delicious young potato or two.

To prepare a dish like hers you should: Grab'l about a quart of the tiny red potatoes. Wash the potatoes and , using an old case knife, SCRAPE all the tender peelings from them. DO NOT peel. Put the potatoes on to boil in approximately 2 C of water and 1/2 tsp of salt. Cook about ten minutes then add:

2-3 C of shelled and washed, very tender

English peas, the kind the Jolly Green Giant
has only dreamed about, but never seen.
3-4 T butter. Now simmer additional 5 minutes. Mix 3 T flour with enough water to make
a thin paste. Add to cooking vegetables—while
stirring—to prevent lumping. Cook 1-2 minutes more. Add 1/2 -1 cup of cream skimmed
from the top of the milk. Heat (do not boil).
This, with hot buttermilk cornbread —like the
fabled "four-and-twenty blackbirds baked in a
pie—'Tis a dainty dish to set before the king."

Do try the following recipes also:

GRANDMA'S COLLARDS
Vera Mae Collins, Northport, AL
In memory of Mary Sullivan

*1 large bunch collards, wash through three
waters.*

5 or 6 bacon slices   *2 T sugar,*
Salt to taste.

Cut collards in medium pieces. Wash,
leave in water temporarily. Fry the bacon—cut
into 2 inch strips—in heavy cooking pot. Now
lift collards to the pot, adding little, if any,
extra water. Cook until well wilted. Add sugar
and salt. Resume cooking until tender. PLAIN,
GOOD EATIN'.

TURNIP GREENS AND
CORNMEAL DUMPLINGS
Loyl Collins, Brookwood, AL

Cook turnip greens with your favorite seasoning—bacon drippings and salt—being careful to add extra water so you will have lots of soup. Remove turnip greens from the pot liquor (pot likker) and keep the liquid hot.

Dumplings:

1 small onion, chopped finely

1/2 tsp of salt   2 C white cornmeal   1 /
4 tsp of pepper, or to taste

Mix all ingredients for dumplings. Add enough boiling water to make the ingredients stick together. Form into small balls and drop into the hot boiling turnip green liquor. Cook gently until dumplings cook through and through, usually about 30 minutes. Serve with turnip greens.

*** I, Faye Brown, would like to inject that my Mama often combined mustard greens and turnip greens from the garden when cooking them. My, was the Pot Likker good! Of course, it always seemed to me that having the wondrous broth in which to soak your cornbread was the real reason for cooking greens in the first place.

When the greens were young and tender in the garden we had to pinch off the tiny leaves or cut them carefully with a small knife. And since steaming the leaves wilts them away to "almost nothing"— well, in order to have a "big mess of greens,", a pot full, we kiddoes had to squat down in the garden for hours, it seemed, "cutting the mustard." It was hard on our legs squatting that way; Granny said we'd have to do it, she was just too old to cut the mustard anymore.

Robert Newman from Fayetteville, TN told me that the above procedure was the basis of an old-timey Square Dance tune, and a subsequent "saying." Said after folks had danced until 10:30 or so at a square dance they would stop for home cooked refreshments. These usually consisted of egg custard or sweet 'tater custard, something which could be held in one's hand and eaten without spoons. Reportedly, just before the recess the dance caller would say, "Swing your partner and do-see-do, hold her hand and round you go, now before we stop and eat the custard, let's everybody squat down and cut the mustard."

That meant, according to Robert, that

everyone should squat down and sit on their heels and bounce around, pretending like they were cutting the mustard greens in the garden for dinner. Now, the young folks could do it but the old folks couldn't; the latter would just stand back and laugh. They were "too old to cut the mustard anymore."

POKE SALAT

Agnes Anders, Northport, AL

Be sure to use only young sprouts (6-8 inches high) of the Poke Salat (or Sallet) plant (which grows wild in the South). Parboil the leaves and sprouts two times, pouring off water after each one-minute boiling. Add water and, the third time, cook the salat until tender. Drain.

Serve the salat "as is" by adding salted bacon drippings and sliced boiled eggs on top. Or fry the poke in bacon drippings and add beaten eggs. Scramble until the beaten eggs are cooked—DELICIOUS!! (You will need good cornbread to go with this.)

From my friend Almeda Dorrah comes similar initial directions for preparing Poke. Then she suggests mixing the cooked poke with cooked turnip greens. Or adding chopped

young onions when frying it down low in bacon
drippings, topping it off with 4 slices of crisply
cooked bacon, crumbled, and the boiled eggs.

SALAD GREENS

My Mama, Pearlie Porter of Northport, AL
fixed the following 'tossed salad' in the early
spring; my Daddy especially loved it.

Gather from the garden, wash, and chop
together in a pyrex dish, approximately:

*1/2 lb each: very young turnip greens amd
    lettuce leaves*

6-8 tender green onions

Set above aside. Fry 2-3 slices bacon or
white meat in skillet. Remove the meat. To the
drippings add 1/2 C water and let simmer a
minute or two. Drizzle the hot liquid over the
fresh greens for a 'dressing.' Add the bacon,
salt and pepper as desired. Serve immediately.

HOPPIN'JOHN

Grace Barrett of Westminster, SC apolo-
gized for running late with this recipe, explaining, "I've been busy as a bee in a tar-bucket."

Cover 1 lb. dried black-eyed peas with 6
C cold water. Bring to a boil; boil two minutes.
Let stand 1 hour. Add 1/2 lb bacon or salt pork

and 2 dried hot red peppers. Simmer about 30 minutes, or until peas are tender, adding more water, if necessary. Cook 2 chopped medium onions in 2 T fat for five minutes. Add to peas with 1 C uncooked rice. Cook, stirring occasionally, until rice is tender. Water should be absorbed. Serves 8.

Let me say, my Mama never prepared peas in this manner. We soaked the dry peas, cooked them with fat back and salt and THAT WAS IT!. We ate them with corn bread and often put pepper sauce or chow-chow on them when eating. Mama'd cook them in a gallon black pot over the fireplace in the winter; the more they were warmed over the better they became. And when they had been cooked so much they became like mush, Mama made Pea Sausage with them (recipe included herein).

CORN ON THE COB

Charlene Pickle, Bishopville,SC

"Some old-timers say it's anticipation of savoring the goodness of corn-on-the-cob that gives them the determination to live through a bitter winter," says Charlene. "It also keeps them spry, because, as they tell it, you have to run fast to prepare it properly. First you put a big pot of water on the stove. While it is getting hot, hurry out to the garden and pick several ears of young, sweet corn. Run back to the kitchen with the corn, shucking the ears and pulling off the silks as you run. Drop the corn into the boiling water and let it cook for a couple o' minutes. As you lift out the steaming ears have plenty of butter and salt ready—plus several big, absorbent napkins. Eat and enjoy!

FRIED CORN

Juanita Hinton Downing, Louisville, KY
Recipe was written down by her mother, Tula Mayhew Hinton (1888-1976) for her children.
2 full C fresh cut corn, white preferred.

2 1/2 C water   1 tsp salt
3 tsp bacon fat
   (or 2 tsp bacon fat and 1 tsp butter)
1/4 tsp black pepper

Mix well and cook on top of stove in heavy vessel. Stir along. After about 20 minutes mix well: 2 rounded T. flour and 1/4 cup sugar in small amount of cold water. Stir slowly into the cooking corn. Taste to see if seasoning is right. Cook slowly 10 minutes longer.
(Modern tip added by Juanita. Packaged frozen cut corn can be used in practically the same way and is very good. First drop the

package into water until thawed. Then proceed as in above recipe. Frozen package of corn has approximately 1 1/2 C cut corn.) ***Faye's note: We called this simply, "Cut-Off corn," as opposed to Fried Corn. And we never added sugar. (Billie Wood, Auburn, AL, shared that her Mom thickens her corn—when necessary—with some grits. Says it works great and since grits come from corn the taste isn't altered.)

CORN FRITTERS

Nona Tindall, St.Cloud, GA

2 C creamed corn   2 eggs
2 C flour

Mix to make a stiff dough. If too stiff add a little milk. Drop by spoonfuls into hot grease. Fry until brown.

MAMA'S SQUASH FRITTERS

Mama made fritters or croquettes similar to the above. Often it was her way of pepping-up leftovers.

2 C stewed squash, cooked low (i.e., most all water evaporated from the squash)

1/4 C chopped onion (better if onion is stewed with the squash)

1 egg, beaten   1/3 C flour

1/2 tsp salt   *1/2 tsp pepper*

Mix together all ingredients., If too dry to hold together add bit of milk. Drop by table-spoonfuls into hot grease in skillet. Cook until brown. Drain.

MAMA'S POTATO CROQUETTES

Substitute 2 C mashed white potatoes for squash, and omit the chopped onion in above Squash Fritters recipe. Then proceed as above with ingredients and cooking directions.

PEA SAUSAGE

Mash up leftover peas (dried or fresh peas) and substitute 2 C mashed peas for squash, omit the chopped onion, then proceed mixing and cooking as with Squash Fritters. I have heard that many families served this for breakfast during The Depression. We were often without real sausage or bacon at our house but Mama never cooked Pea Sausage for breakfast. We DID, however, love it for dinner or supper on cold days. Mama often moistened the batter with pea soup or water because the eggs had all been exchanged for flour and coffee at the rolling store.

MAMA'S FRIED GREEN TOMATOES

4-6 medium green tomatoes (better if very green, firm -not showing any pink), sliced 1/4-1/3 inch thick

1 C flour (Our neighbors coated theirs with cornmeal, not us.)

salt to sprinkle   black pepper (optional)

lard (or bacon drippings, cooking oil)

Have your lard hot in a thick skillet. Sprinkle slices with salt, and pepper if desired. Coat each tomato slice with flour and drop into the hot grease. Fry tomatoes, turning, until lightly browned on each side. Drain. Great served with Mama's Homemade Catsup.

MAMA'S BAKED OKRA-GREEN TOMATOES

Cut approximately 2 lbs of okra into 3/4 inch slices. Chop 3-4 medium, extra-firm green tomatoes into medium-sized cubes. Mix. Sprinkle with 1 T. of salt. Then coat with 1/3 C flour, 2/3 C cornmeal. Heat on top of stove: 3-5 T of lard (shortening, oil) in an extra large oblong pan or oven proof dish. Pour okra-tomatoes into the sizzling grease, turn over or stir gently after 1 minute. Continue to brown for 2-3 minutes. Then place into hot (400 degree) oven. Bake for approximately 1 hour, turning carefully occasionally. Avoid burning and "turning into hash" with excessive stirring.

POTATO SOUP
Dorothy Gast, Coker, AL

2 medium potatoes   1 C water
2 green onions or 1 dry onion 1 C milk
1/4 C butter   1 tsp salt
Black pepper to taste

Peel and cube potatoes and add to salted water. Add chopped onions and cook until potatoes are tender. Add butter and milk and simmer 5 minutes. Serve with your favorite crackers.

Dorothy said, "My Mama Annice used to fix this for us when we were sick. Or had it ready to serve when we were coming home from school on a cold day. It is a regular comfort food."

*** FAYE's Conclusion: If you happen to spy me in the produce department of the grocery store or down at the curb market—and I'm meticulously going through the peas, picking out the tiny yellow squash, sorting out the very tiniest potatoes. Well, I don't mean to be selfish or picky. I just can't help it; I inherited from Mama this thing about young, tender veggies. And there's no steak dinner on earth that I'd prefer over a 'Veggie-Night' of tender creamed corn, oven-fried okra, tiny green limas, vine-ripened tomatoes, chow-chow, and hot corn bread. In fact, this is the meal that my sisters and I refer to as "THE Meal," and I could eat it every night for a Month-O-Sundays.

Hoppin' A Ride With
The Mail Rider

The mail rider was much more than a stranger who delivered mail for the U.S. Government when I was a youngun'. In our neck of the woods the feller who stopped at our mailbox was a special friend, loved like family, and for good reason,too. Being one of a rare breed who was able to afford an automobile, car tires, and gasoline during the Great Depression—and one of a special group who was entitled to purchase them during WW II, this carrier of the mail was often, during summer week-a-days, the only one who ventured into the outside world and brought us back a bit of it.

Mama would rush from cooking the dinner to wait by the mailbox, hurry when she recognized the mail rider's old Ford beginning its long grinding climb up the mountain from the Courington's.

As soon as the caring gentleman handed Mama a letter, saying, "Looks like you've got word from your sister in Northport, Mrs.Porter," he'd count out the penny-postcards in return for the nickel she offered.

Then the kind man would pass the time of day with Mama, asking how everybody was doing, He'd tell, excitedly, that the Ledbetters who lived over past the creek had a new baby boy, the spittin' image of Mr. Ledbetter, and that both mama and baby were peart. Mr. Willcutt had been bitten by a huge rattler, while cutting logs. And they'd taken him all the way to Tuscaloosa to the hospital; still didn't know if he was gonna make it. After adding that " Miz Watkins is stove up with rheumatiz, but doing tolerable," he finally bade "Good day" and drove off in a cloud of dust down the gravel road.

Mama'd ring the dinner bell five minutes early. She could hardly wait till Daddy and we kids washed up, gathered at the table, and had Grace before she spilled all the news the mailman'd shared. Plus the good tidings from Aunt Margaret that her hen had just hatched out ten baby chicks and five little ducklings, to boot. " 'Spect that mama hen'll be up the creek without a paddle, when those ducks start takin' to the branch,"

Mama rared back and laughed. We all joined in; the mail rider had, once again, made our day.

We often left three coppers on top of an addressed envelope in the mail box; the accommodating mailman licked and attached the stamp, sending the letter on its way. Or lacking even an envelope during Depression Days, we have been known to leave the necessary pennies and place a folded letter to Grandma, written on tablet paper, along with a forwarding address on a scrap of brown poke. Place the unfinished items in the little roadside metal box and raise the flag; the mail rider would address a stamped envelope and godspeed it on to Grandma, without even a grunt.

When Mama made up the order blank to Sears, Roebuck for a dollar remnant bundle and a thirty-nine cent package of one hundred and fifty Valentines, she had us leave it at the mailbox. The neighborly postman took it into the post office, purchased the money order for us and next day returned the change—or else he had a money order with him and performed the transaction on the spot.

On days when we were receiving a wonderful big cattylog, or when a package was arriving with a pair of brogans for Daddy, or a box of 50 little baby chicks was to be delivered—when something big and important was coming the mail rider would begin blowing his horn as he left the previous box, two miles away. It took a diplomatic Mama to decide which excited kid was gonna leave their chores, that time, to meet the mailman.

Our honorable letter carrier often broke the government's rules because he was such a sympathetic soul. Seeing Daddy heading out a'foot on a freezing day— walking to town to talk to the doctor about a sick child—the mail rider would stop and give him a ride in his brand-spanking new car. And once when Daddy was sick Mama just sent a note to the druggist by the obliging feller. The mailman's sounding horn the following day gave Mama the cue to run and meet him; he had, indeed, gone the second mile—had brought a bottle of medicine from the drugstore.

Our mail rider was not alone in his helpful spirit. "You jest never seen the beat 'o Mr. George Hardin in all ye born days," the folks up in the Brookwood community say to this day, referring to the former mailman who lived among them to the bright age of 102. As one who first began delivering the mail over muddy cow trails with a horse and buggy, the obliging individual saw many changes in the postal service during his lifetime. And back when times were hard and folks needed a helping hand, he always tried to lend one.

Mr. Hardin related this story to me: " It was during the Great Depression. A feller who was gravely ill was told by the doctor the only thing that would prolong his life was to have fresh ground raw beef three times a week. The rural family had no car, no refrigerator, no way of providing the necessary meat during the hot summer. Someone mentioned it to me and we worked it out. The butcher in the grocery next door to the post office would get the meat ready, early, three mornings a week. And after getting the mail for delivery loaded into my car I would rush in, get the vital package, and deliver it to the home as I made my run. I did it for several months, until the poor man died. It was against the rules, but they needed the help and I was glad to do it," the humble gentleman told.

Mr. Hardin remembered, also, a fellow mailman who got reprimanded by his superior for being helpful to country folk. Seems the mail rider had a sack of shorts loaded into his trunk one day, destined for a farmer's pigs. Suddenly the inspector showed up, to ride that day with the letter carrier. The feller was undaunted, however; when he reached the friend's home he stopped the car, got out, took the heavy sack of feed, and placed it on the front porch.

As the postman and his passenger pulled away from the mailbox, the mail inspector remarked, "Was there any postage on that sack of feed?" "Well, no," the helpful carrier replied, "but during this long, wet winter I've been stuck on that muddy hill back there about ten times. And that farmer has brought his plow horses and pulled me over the hill, or outta the ditch every single time. And there's never been any postage on that either." And, according to Mr. Hardin, that was the end of the inspector's sarcastic reprisal.

My friend Eva recalls that Mr. Hardin had a tender spot in his heart for his young daughter, Loyl, many years ago also. And, once in a great while, when Loyl and her little friend Eva would beg and beg, Mr. Hardin would "give in" and let the two of them ride along on his route, provided they promised to be good, sit quietly, and not touch the mail.

Another senior acquaintance recently revived memories of her family's helpful mail rider. Said, "Every week he'd pick up a sack of shelled corn from our house and drop it off at the grist mill. A day or so later there he'd be, at mail time, with the ground meal, ready for our cornbread."

And another told of her mom, who didn't know how to shoot a gun—of her rushing out and summoning the mailman to use their shotgun and kill a rattlesnake in the yard. Then there was the story of a young child being returned home from their aunt's, during a big snow, via the mailman; seemed the aunt paid the postage due on the small lad. One lady "took the cake" when she shared that she and her hubby were married by a mailman who was also a minister of the Gospel; he just paused alongside the road one day, had the couple pledge "I DO" and went on his way.

Yep, long ago mail carriers were such good friends. And rural folks, in turn, were good to them. I recall Mama having us run out to the mailbox in the early spring with a mess of fresh picked Kentucky Wonder beans for Mr. Elmore. Or some grabled new red potatoes. Or a quart of blackberries, just fresh from the morning dew. Summers it was roas'nears; falls it was sweet 'taters that we shared with our mailman. Sometimes the offerings were left inside the mailbox, away from the weather or the animals.

Agnes shared a story about her father, the mailman, and some food in a mailbox. Seems a farmer, plowing near the road, deposited his lunch in the mailbox one day, protection against ants and dogs. The mailman came early that morning, was surprised,and remarked to himself, "Well, how thoughtful of the Jones' to pack me this picnic." He drove a mile or so, found himself a shady spot and proceeded to enjoy the ham biscuits, the boiled eggs, and the piece of fresh pound cake wrapped in waxed paper. Seems, however, that the puzzled farmer got mighty hungry and weak before sundown that day.

When that hungry farmer thought about the situation, however, he knew what had happened—and not without foundation, either. Because his family, like ours and most others during the 'good ole days,' had a loving and sharing relationship with the postman. It was no wonder most felt so close we would gladly have given him our lunch; the feller acommodated us by carrying our corn, our medicine, our sick to the doctor. Instead of being only a mail carrier, the feller who brought letters when I was a child could more appropriately have been called "an everything carrier." How is it that saying goes... "Neither pig feed, snakes, nor Holy Matrimony...shall stay the mail?"

Don't Come Totin' No Kentucky Fried When You're Settin' Up With The Dead

A few years back I had a fringe affiliation, of which I'm not proud, with a group who voted to order Kentucky Fried Chicken, cole slaw, and baked beans whenever a death occurred within their circle; they refused to be bothered with preparing and delivering food to the home of the bereaved. Such disrespect was unheard of long-ago in our neck of the woods. Why, wringing a chicken's neck and cooking up a big pot of chicken-

dumplin's or baking a scrumptious caramel cake
was one way a woman individualized her sympathy to the sorrowin' back when I was a kid.

Of course, people were closer to death and
dying back then, didn't try to deny it by prettying
it up, by letting strangers take care of their sick,
their dead. I was a wee lass when my Grandpa
Porter was so sick, with what we now know as
cancer. It didn't matter that it was in the "sprang
of th' year" and the farmers put in killing days
behind their two-muled break plows. After their
wives had come and helped Granny and Aunt
Gertrude wait on the sick during the day, the
neighboring men poured in to "set up with Mr.
Bill," night after night.

They were sleepin' and settin' in shifts the
night he died. Mr. Gurley Pugh was grabbing a few
winks down at our house, next door to Grandpap's,
before he and my Daddy Ira planned to sit during
the last watch. But then the terrible storm hit.
Blew our little house away; blew half the country
away, damaged Grandpap's house, blew down
one chimney— yet didn't even ruffle the curtains
in the room where he lay at death's door. Folks
said it beat all they'd ever seen.

In spite of all the devastation and folks
having more to do at their own place than they

could shake a stick at, Grandpap hadn't drawn
his last breath more'n a couple 'o hours when the
word had traveled and the place was "wropped
up" with friends and neighbors, men volunteering
to help build the coffin, dig the grave, or just stand
around with my Dad and his sorrowing brothers—just stand around with their heads bowed.
(Still others were down at the foot of the hill trying
to improvise a bridge so folks could get through.
Seems the WPA had the old bridge torn out for
replacement when the disaster struck.)

And the womenfolk—for two straight days—
came bearing precious gifts of food. Lulabelle
brought a ham pie, a molasses cake, sweep potato
cobbler; Mae, her homemade light bread, a pot of
dried butterbeans, and a pone of crackling bread,
which together must have taken her eight hours
to prepare. Ollie had, looked like, nearly a dishpan full 'uh chicken 'n dressing made with "the
fattest hen I had, what had quit laying." Lillie,
remembering that my just-widowed Granny loved
poke salat, went into the woods and gathered
some tender sprouts of the wild plant. She stewed
it, then fried it down and scrambled some eggs in
it for Granny. And on and on they brought their
expressions of love, of sympathy to feed the large
family which gathered to mourn.

It was no different when other country folk 'WENT HOME' back then. I remember my best friend's grandma's death. Men and women who'd been there sitting when she passed over—well, they fanned out to notify the entire countryside. One feller went out back and rang the dinner bell, rang it real slowly, rang it ninty-four times—one for each of her years.

The good women came quickly to help bathe her and "lay her out." They didn't have to worry about sending into town to the Yellow Front for cloth to quickly sew a shroud, however. The dear old lady had made her own burying clothes and put 'em back twenty odd years before. Mama said lotta the ladies were shaking their heads 'cause she'd made a light pink garment instead of the usual black one. (Not much different from today's personalized, pre-arranged funeral plans, I don't reckon.)

But they did send for black cloth to cover the outside and white broadcloth to line the simple pine wood casket which the neighboring men made quickly. While they were down at Mr. Jones' shop sawing and hammering, the women got 'grandma' dressed quickly, before she got too stiff to work with, " 'fore the rigor mortis sets in," then kept her cool as possible—kept laying wet rags over her face to keep it from turning dark since they wasn't able to "git her mortified." They laid nickels over her eyes to keep them closed; would've used silver half-dollars or quarters if they'd have had 'em, anything 'cept copper, which might turn 'er green. They 'uz determined to put 'er away nice.

For two days the work on the surrounding farms ceased. Men did what they could and women slaved over their wood stoves, turning out their very best 'vittles' for the family that was hurting: fried chicken, brunswick stew, green beans with new potatoes, squash patties, fried apple pies and bread pudding.

'Grandma' was placed in the homemade casket, the bed she'd died in was taken down and they turned the room into a parlor for the wake. Since my friend was close to her granny and I was close to my friend I was permitted to stay overnight. They's so many folks stayed and slept over til they almost had to get one t'sleep, stand 'em in the corner, then let another lay down. Why, up't thirty folks, I'd say, just lingered, visiting, 'til atter midnight. They'd walk, like my friend and I did, in and out of the room and look, sadly, at the deceased laying there with the piece of cheese-cloth over the top of the box to keep, one said, "the flies and the cats offen her."

As my young friend and I sat quietly, reflec-
tively, on the porch's edge that summer night we
overheard two men talking quietly under the
trees, telling about setting up with the dead long
before. One related this story: He and three other
strapping youths were settin' up with their friend
who'd died from a snake bite; had been bitten
while they were all down at the creek, fishing.
Well, there they were in the room with the casket
which was covered with a sheet to keep off insects.
When, lo and behold, about two in the morning
the sheet started moving up and down, up and
down.

The story teller said at first he just glared,
wide-eyed, but then he LIT OUT! Flew out of that
room, that house, headed home as fast as his legs
would carry him. And after awhile he heard, " pit,
pat, pit ..." behind him, gaining, closer and closer;
he was sure it was the friend's ghost!

Reaching home he jumped onto the porch,
knocking over a barrel of corn, and scaring the old
dog who, in turn, could be heard howling a mile
away. The "pit, pat" arrived also, and it turned out
to be the second, and the third, scared friends—
boys alive, but not too well. The man related that
his awakened father listened to their story and

went to the dead's home to have a look-see, himself. He discovered: A CAT HAD SOMEHOW GOTTEN UNDER THE SHEET AND WAS MOV- ING UP AND DOWN, desperately trying to escape. (By the way— Mr. Tindall said he never, never again saw hair nor hide 'uv his old dog.)

Seems that, most often, the cats were the culprits. As in this story which Mr. Albert Elzie Lee recently shared: Ladies were sitting up with a corpse, when he was a youngun'. 'Bout two, three in the morning—just at the time when ghost are most active—well, the curtains in the room started moving, and an unusual noise was heard. Now it being in the dead of winter the windows were closed, no air currents, no explanations. Yet the curtains kept moving, the noise kept 'a-coming. The women hated to admit they were 'bout scared outta their skins when they went, breathless, into the kitchen where some folks were keeping the coffee pot going. A few brave men ventured, found only a cat behind the curtains, playing with a brown paper poke.

My Daddy told this 'setting-up-with-the-dead-story' which left cats out altogether. It goes: An old lady died who'd been very, very humped in her back; had walked with her head bent over past her waist. Those who helped lay her out, put

her into the casket, took an old inner tube from a
Model-T and cut it into pieces. Then they forced
the lady's body to lie flat in the box, holding her
down with the rubber strips across her chest, and
groin, and tacked on either side to the box. With
her full shroud on, no one who came to view her
suspected anything. Just stood there saying how
"good she looked" and "... ain't it a mir'cle how,
when she died, her back finally relaxed to let her
lie flat, in peace."

It was nearing nine o'clock when folks started
offering to stay over, to "set up with the dead."
When Purvis said to Henry, "Well, if you're gonna
set up, I'm leaving." Awhile later Leon remarked
to Jake, "I'd be glad to stay, but if you're gonna set
up, I'm leaving." And so it went, until most had
gone home, the family had gone to bed, and only
two were left settin' up with the dead.

It was just after midnight. All was quiet and
a little eerie as Ole Jake and Henry sat there
alone, dozing just a little every now and then,
almost as relaxed as the corpse. They,
incidentially, knew nothing of the real story behind Miss Lila's relaxation. When all of a sudden,
"POP, POW, POP" rang through the stillness,
causing the men to jump upright, take notice.
Upon seeing Miss Lila sitting upright in her coffin,

they hollered out, "MISS LILA, IF YOU'RE SETTIN' UP, WE'RE LEAVING!" They ran the five miles to their homes without so much as a glance backwards! After the funeral, as the tales of Miss Lila's ghost circulated the community, the nerve-wrecked men were greatly relieved to hear the truth—how the rotted rubber strips had snapped, first one and then the other, releasing the bent body.

From my in-laws comes the experience of Jack and Howard. Left alone in the room of an old house with a dead man in a casket about 3 AM the two were almost overcome with sleep. Jack could stand it no longer; he went into the next room for a short nap. Howard tried to keep his eyes open, hoping to switch places with Jack shortly. Half dozing, half dreaming he sat... when suddenly...he thought he saw...down the sloping floor of the room the casket-on-wheels began shifting... moving... rolling...flying! "JACK, JACK," the then wide-awake Howard screamed, "JACK, HE'S LEAVING US, HE'S LEAVING US...!"

Yea, Albert Lee knows a lot of good dead-folks tales. He remembers, at the age of twelve, driving his Granny in a buggy to call on a family whose daddy was barely hanging on; back home his granny described the feller's condition, "He's dead all but shutting his mouth." He related this also: "Once a preacher was preaching the funeral of a dead boy named Willie. In the congregation sat the deceased's father and his mentally retarded brother. Well, the minister just raved on-and-on about the wonderful things Willie had done in this life." (Preacher wasn't taking into account the feller's faults. Like my Aunt Veenie'd say—"Everything that goes over the Devil's back comes under his belly, buckled down tight." Or, in plain language, "Your sins are gonna find you out; the devil gets his due.") Well, according to Albert the reverend continued bragging about Willie's terrific contributions. Finally the son, who didn't know to always "saint-ti-fy all dead," called out, disrupting the funeral, "PA, GO UP THERE AND LOOK IN THAT BOX. THAT CAN'T BE WILLIE! WILLIE 'UZ MEANER I AM."

Mr. Lee also told me how, following his great-grandpa's funeral, they were taking his body to the burying. Taking him to the cemetery in a wagon, a wagon missing its tailgate. As they were nearing the appointed place—the men dressed in suits wearing black armbands and the women all in black, walking reverently behind — well they came to a steep little incline. The gently prodding mules suddenly lurched forward and the coffin slid square dab outta the back 'o the wagon. Hit the ground a'bounchin', bounced the pore dead soul right outta the box, I believe the story goes.

Albert 'lows, " lotta folks are skeedish about ANY LITTLE OLE THANG that has to do with the dead. One feller had him a boarding place over at Thrasher Cut; a nice place, only one problem. Every night while he was trying to get a little shut-eye Uncle Josh was out back in his shop hammering on coffins. Making caskets for th'dead and dying all the time, all day 'n all night. The noise wadn't what kept Old Man John Webb awake, it was the idea of it that spooked 'im; couldn't bear the thought of Josh always making boxes to bury folks in. SO HE LEFT! One day just upped and moved, left his nice place 'account 'uh 'th box building."

In a lot of ways that feller was, I think, like most folks today, wanting to bury their heads in the sand and pretend like dying don't happen, not wantin' t' involve themselves in it. When somebody dies the most they gonna do is pick up the phone and call some catering service to send a little fast food to the home of the bereaved, or wire a FTD bouquet of flowers for the funeral, or run by the funeral home for two minutes—sign the book,

Ohhhhhh and Awwwww over all the pretty wreaths, then head home. Even heard of one new fangled drive-by funeral home where you can just drive by and say your goodbys, guess you could go in your night gown if you'uz lazy enough.

Sure a lot different from when I was a kid. Like one old timer told me, "Back then they'd lay ye out, build yer coffin, dig yer grave, brang their best vittles ...all to show their love 'n respect. Now when ye die they don't give a hang whether ye live or die."

I'm here to warn you. I've spent my best years writing these stories for you to enjoy. Now when I've passed—and folks are here, settin' up with the dead—don't you dare come totin' no microwaveable entree or no jiffy Kentucky Fried! You think enough of my memory to slave over that hot stove for a while. Or at least go to Miss Melissa's great little cafe in Moundville, Alabama and get her to fix one of her renowed Caramel Cakes for you to bring. Else I'm li'bl'st to hop right outta that ole pine box and sic a dozen scary cats on ye as ye come through the door!

Childhood Cakes: Dried Apple Stack Cakes, Jelly Rolls Etc.

MAMA'S EVER'DAY CAKE

Pearlie Maebell Shirley Porter, Northport, AL

When we were busy in the fields and someone had a birthday, or else Mama just decided we needed a "little something extra" at dinner, Mama quickly cooked this "ever'day , or plain cake," as she called it. We, however, always felt it was great, "company come to town," especially when she added the custard on top.

2 C flour (recipe adjusted for self-rising)

1/2 C butter   1 C sugar

1 egg   1 tsp vanilla

1/2 C milk

Mix all together and bake in oblong cake pan, 30-35 minutes in a 4-stick-stovewood

(350 degree) oven. Cut in squares and serve while hot, as is, or with warm custard topping.

AUNT BERT'S
PINEAPPLE UPSIDE DOWN CAKE

The foregoing basic recipe may be turned into a Pineapple Upside Down Cake. Simply put 1/2 C brown sugar, 1 small can of sliced pineapple with juice, and 4 T butter into bottom of oblong pan. Heat until butter melts. Pour the Ever'day Cake batter into pan and cook as above. Remove cake from pan while still hot.

If the Pineapple Upside Down Cake is so good you "just can't stand it" then you'll know that it's just like my Aunt Bert Brown's was long ago. I'd always stay a night or two with her, Uncle Bud, and their two oldest younguns—Mackey and Nancy—during the summers long ago. I thought she was one of the best cooks in the world—because she occasionally opened aluminum cans from the store and she served those delicious Pork 'n Beans just like they came out of the can. And hers was the first Pineapple Upside Down Cake I ever ate; never in all the ensuing years have I tasted better.

MAMA'S COTTAGE PUDDING
or Custard Topping

2 C whole milk	l C sugar
1 egg	l tsp vanilla
1 T flour	

Stir sugar, flour, and milk together. Cook over low heat, stirring constantly until it begins to thicken. Beat egg and add to cooking mixture gradually, to prevent lumping. Cook 2-3 minutes longer. Remove from heat, add vanilla. Beat until smooth. Spoon hot over cake and serve. Or pour into small dishes and allow to cool before serving as pudding.

Following is a great filling for a plain cake like the one above of my Mama's. However, when we were growing up we referred to any such topping as 'icing', whether it soaked into the cake, was placed between layers, or glazed the top of the cake.

BUTTERMILK FILLING:
FOR HIKKER NUT CAKES, OTHERS
(At least 50 years old)
Opal Broughton, Northport, AL

l C buttermilk	2 C sugar
1/2 lb. butter (or oleo)	

Mix all together. Cook over medium heat until syrup will spin a thread when poured from a spoon.

Add 1 tsp vanilla and mix.

Add 1/2 tsp baking soda and mix vigorously, until it appears glossy. Add chopped nuts if desired. Spread on baked cake layers.

(You will need my Mama's Ever'day Cake and Opal's filling to make my Granny's Hikker Nut Cake.)

When Mama wanted to really make her Ever'day Cake special, as when she was taking it to Hannah's Methodist Church on the Second Sunday in May for the 'All Day Dinner and Singing on the Ground'— as we kids referred to the occasion —well, then she made this Caramel Icing to go between the layers, and to completely cover the outside of the cake. (Seemed that while I's eatin' this caramel cake I'd always be thinkin' on the struggle it'd been gettin' Ole Bossy to let down her milk, with me having to pull and pull on her little bitty ole tits, while she switched me in the face with her big tail full of 'cuckle-burrs'.)

CARAMEL FROSTING
Pearlie Shirley Porter

3 cups sugar   *1 cup cream skimmed*
from top of milk

Melt 1/2 C of the sugar in a heavy skillet. Stir almost constantly until it becomes a golden brown (do not scorch).

Meanwhile, put 2 1/2 C of the sugar in a saucepan with the milk. Bring to a boil. Pour the golden browned sugar into the mixture. (While it is just to the boiling stage.) Cook to softball stage. Remove from heat. Beat until creamy. Frost cake.

My Aunt Gertrude Porter has been known for miles around, years on end, for her famous caramel frosted cakes. She and my Mama used the same method of caramelizing the sugar and cooking the frosting. However, Aunt Gertrude recently gave me her modernized ingredient list:

3 C sugar, 1 C homogenized (whole) milk, plus 2 T oleo.

MAMA'S JELLY ROLL
A wonderful treat that Mama often made late on Saturday afternoons was a Jelly Roll, two jelly rolls, in fact. Sometimes she would

just spread jelly on her Ever'day Cake (see foregoing recipe). But to make a 'roll' with it, she baked it like Louise's, following, and usually doubled the recipe.

JELLY ROLL
Louise House, Brookwood, AL

3 eggs	1 tsp baking powder
1 C sugar	1/3 tsp salt
1 C flour	1 (16 oz) jar jelly/jam
2 T cold water	

Mama would let part of us younguns beat the eggs and sugar til our wrists were tired. Other kids would be busy sifting, then re-sifting the flour, salt, and baking powder together —getting it all over ourselves and the cabinet counter and the floor. The water and dry mixture would then be added—first a bit of one and then a bit of the other—to the egg-sugar mixture, till all was used up and beaten very smoothly. Then we would line one, or two, shallow pans (10" x 15", or regular jelly roll pans) with waxed paper—being very frugal with the cherished paper.

Mama would next pour the batter into the pans and spread it out good with the spoon. She would always leave a bit more of the batter than was necessary in the bowl for us kids to scrape; and let the little ones sit in the middle of the floor and enjoy scraping and scraping and licking the spoons til it seemed that even the bowl might be completely scraped away.

Then she would put the cakes to bake in a pretty hot oven. If you're cooking in your Home Comfort woodstove you're gonna need more than corncobs to heat with, gonna take about a 5-sticks-of-stovewood-oven (Modern terms, preheated-400 degree) for approximately 20 minutes. Mama would cook until a straw from the top of the broom could be inserted into the cake and come out clean. Warning us to stay back a bit, Mama then turned the cakes out onto clean flour sacks spread with granulated sugar (powdered sugar is better, but we only had that once while I was growing up.)

While the cakes were still a bit warm—not too hot—Mama would gently pull the waxed paper from the back of the cake. Then we would vie to help spread each with scrumptious homemade jelly —scuppernong, muscadine, or apple. Mama would gently roll them up, then roll the flour sack around one of them-not tight enough to let it steam—but tight enough to hold it in its roll. Hide it in the pie safe for Sunday Dinner (while making sure none of those tiny little ants were crawling around to notify an entire ant army to "come and git it.")

Then came PAYDAY! Mama would slice the second jelly roll while it was still hot and reward us waiting kids for not jumping around and making the cake fall while it was cooking. And give a slice to Daddy who'd just be coming in from the grist mill with the freshly ground cornmeal. What a wonderful close it was to a hard week; our family all sitting around the table eating our good hot jelly roll off the delicate pink saucers which we'd gotten out of the oatmeal boxes.

PLAIN POUND CAKE
From Louise House, Brookwood, AL
Inherited recipe from Hattie Toxey

6 eggs	2 C flour
2 C sugar	2 tsp baking powder
1 C butter (or shortening)	1 tsp flavoring

Cream sugar and butter (or shortening). Add eggs, one at a time. Beat well after each egg. Add flour, baking powder, and flavoring. Pour into tube pan. Bake in 325 degree oven for one hour or until done.

SPONGE CAKE (over 100 years old)

Annie Northen, Shreveport, LA

FAYES NOTE: This recipe, like the "Calves' Feet Jelly" in the Breakfast section, was a page torn from a 1892 cookbook which belonged to Annie Northen's mother-in-law. I only wish I could have shared with you the original page and it's fascination; but here's the recipe, verbatim, in true form:

"One pound sugar, one of flour, ten eggs. Stir yolks of eggs and sugar till perfectly light; beat whites of eggs and add them with the flour after beating together lightly; flavor with lemon. three teaspoons baking powder in the flour will add to its lightness, but it never fails without. Make in a moderate oven."

IRISH POTATO CAKE

(Over 150 years old)

Zelda Lawrence, Coker, AL

(Obtained from Lucille Hendrix)

3 eggs, well beaten
1 1/2 tsp baking powder
1 C cooked irish potatoes, finely mashed.

1 C dark raisins	1 1/2 C sugar
1/2 C butter	1/2 C grated chocolate
2 C flour	3/4 C sweet milk

Cream butter and sugar. Add beaten eggs. Add flour and baking powder alternately with milk. Add other ingredients, mix well. Pour in greased and floured tube pan. Bake at 350 degrees for 50-60 minutes.

FIG CAKE

Aileen Kilgore Henderson, Brookwood, AL
Inherited from her Mom.

l C self-rising flour, sifted	1 C sugar
1/4 C melted butter	1/2 C milk
1/2 tsp vanilla extract	Pinch salt
2 eggs	1 pint fig preserves, mashed.

Sift together flour, sugar, and salt. Add milk and blend. Add butter, vanilla extract, eggs and figs. Mix well. Pour into a greased 9 x 7 x 2 inch pan. Bake at 350 degrees for 30 to 45 minutes or until cake is done. It will be a bit waxy. Cut in squares while still in pan. Serve warm with whipped cream, ice cream, or hard sauce.

BLACK WALNUT CAKE

Aileen Kilgore Henderson, Brookwood, AL

1/2 C butter	2 C flour
2 C brown sugar	1/2 tsp salt
3 egg yolks, beaten	1 tsp vanilla extract

3 tsp baking powder   3 egg whites, beaten

2/3 C milk

1 C black walnuts, chopped fine or ground.

Cream butter. Add sugar and beat until smooth. Add beaten egg yolks and mix well. Combine dry ingredients and add to creamed mixture alternately with milk. Add vanilla and walnuts. Mix well. Fold in stiffly beaten egg whites. Bake in greased tube pan at 350 degrees for 45 minutes.

MAMA'S JAM CAKE

Rovine Cunningham, Brookwood, AL

3 C flour	2 C sugar
4 eggs	1 C butter or oleo
1 C buttermilk	1 tsp. baking soda
1/2 tsp cinnamon	1/4 tsp cloves
1/4 tsp nutmeg	1 C blackberry jam

Stir baking soda into buttermilk; set aside. In large bowl cream butter and sugar until light and fluffy. Add eggs, one at a time; beat well. In medium bowl combine flour and spices. Add dry ingredients alternately with buttermilk to egg mixture, beginning and ending with flour. Stir in jam. Bake at 350 degrees until done. Ice cake layers with your favorite frosting.

DRIED APPLE CAKE

Rovine Cunningham, Brookwood, AL

1 C butter	2 C sugar
3 eggs	1 tsp vanilla
1 C buttermilk	2 1/2 C sifted flour
1/2 tsp salt	1 tsp baking soda

Cream butter and sugar until fluffy; add eggs one at a time and beat well. Add vanilla. Sift together: flour, salt and soda. Add dry ingredients alternately with buttermilk to butter mixture, beating after each addition, until smooth. Pour into 3 greased and floured pans. Bake at 350 degrees for 30-40 minutes. Cool before frosting.

FROSTING: 2 C stewed dried apples, sweetened to taste, 1 cup grated coconut, 1 tsp vanilla. Mix three ingredients well. Frost the cool layers. (Home dried apples give a better flavor.) Let cake set in a tightly covered container for 12 hours before cutting to enhance flavor.

NOTE FROM FAYE: Mama made an "apple stack cake" like this at times, except she used only dried apples and sugar to stack hers with. The cake was delicious! Mama's recipe came from Aunt Beck Hannah, my Granny Porter's sister. Aunt Beck's recipe for the "cake" part was like a rich cookie, and she baked 5-6 very thin layers on her iron baker, in her wood stove. After stacking, Aunt Beck stored her cake in the pie safe for a day or so before serving. In her cold house it needed no refrigeration in the winter. At our house the cake was eaten so quickly it needed no refrigeration even in the summer! Aunt Beck's cake was similar to the one below.

APPLE STACK CAKE

Carol Henry from Wyandotte, Michigan, sent this recipe from her Tennessee childhood. Says she has introduced this cake and fried half-moon apple pies to her northern neighbors —and they now love them like Southern folks have long done!

5-6 C self-rising flour	2 C sugar
2 whole eggs, beaten	1 C buttermilk
1/2 C butter	1/2 C shortening
1 T vanilla	

Sift 4 C flour into large mixing bowl. Make a "well" in the center. Pour in sugar, beaten eggs, shortening, butter, and vanilla. Add buttermilk, gradually working all ingredients into flour (using hand is the best way to mix). Add more flour to mixture until a stiff

dough is formed. Chill about 30 minutes.

In greased and floured, preferably round, cake pans, place a small ball of the dough... enough to make an approximate 1/2 inch thick layer after it is baked. Spread the dough out thinly to the edges of the pans by pressing with hand. Bake at 350 degrees for about 12 minutes or until golden brown. Remove from pan and cool. Repeat until dough is used up; should make 9-11 layers.

When cool stack with cooked sweetened home-dried apples. When last layer is in place, put apples on top of and around outside edges of the layers to seal cake completely. Store in refrigerator for 2-3 days before serving. The longer it sets, the better it becomes.

MAMA'S APPLE STACK CAKE
Doris Leavelle, Austin, TX
(From her Mama, Lydia Ann Stephens
Henderson in Alabama before 1940, Doris
shares this, yet another version of the cake
found in many folks' memories.)

3/4 C lard (or shortening)	4 C flour
1 C sugar	1/2 tsp soda
1 C molasses	1 tsp salt
3 eggs	1 C milk

At least 3 C thickly stewed applesauce

    Cream shortening and add sugar, a little at a time, blending well. Add molasses and mix thoroughly. Add eggs, one at a time, beating well after each addition. Add milk alternately with the sifted dry ingredients. Beat until smooth. Place mixture about 3/8 inch deep in six 9-inch greased, floured pans. Bake at 375 degrees for 18-20 minutes. When cool, stack up layers, using the stewed and sweetened home-dried 'applesauce' generously between layers. After the cake sits 2-3 hours it is very moist and delicious! (Doris says she often cooks this cake in three layers, then slices them, making a total of six layers.)

And a special dessert —not a cake but:

MAMA'S BUTTER ROLL

Elizabeth Dean Akridge, Coker, AL

2 C flour	*3/4 to 7/8 C buttermilk*
1/2 tsp soda 1/2 tsp salt	
1/2 C shortening (scant)	
2 C sugar	*1 1/2 C hot water*
1 tsp vanilla OR 1/2 tsp nutmeg	
2 C warm milk	

    Mix together flour, soda, and salt. Cut in shortening and add milk enough to make a dough you can roll. Divide dough in half and roll each piece on a floured cloth to about the thickness of pie crust. Spread each circle with soft butter and sprinkle with 1/2 cup of the sugar on each piece.

Roll up, jelly-roll fashion, and cut into 1 1/2 inch slices. Place slices in deep baking dish. Place the remaining butter and the remaining cup of sugar over the rolls. Add the vanilla or nutmeg. Pour the warm milk and hot water, mixed, over the rolls and bake in a 350 degree oven for about 45 minutesm until the rolls are brown and the syrup is thick.

FAYE'S NOTE: Long ago when my Mama made this delicious butter roll we realized God had blessed us in the manner the wise man had prayed for in Proverbs 30:8-9 with neither poverty nor great riches, but had blessed us "just perfectly."

Riding The Rails With Hobo Joe

This morning I walked the stones' throw to the railroad tracks; watching from my window would not satisfy. I was drawn by the modern machinery which was taking up a quarter-mile of old track and replacing it with new in a matter of minutes. Reworking the same amount of track fifty years ago would have taken "slave-labor" from an entire crew of men for days on end.

My observations today weren't as exciting as when track repairing had more of a human touch, when the hard labor was performed to the beat of a rhythm. When a "caller" sang or lead in songs to help a repair gang work more steadily and to keep folks from smashing each other's hands and heads with the huge hammers.

Most of my childhood was spent on farms far removed from fascinating railroad tracks; the wind and temperature had to be "just right" for us to hear a train, even while we sat on the porch after work. For our ears to pick up the lonesome wail of the steam locomotive as it wound in the midnight darkness around the mountainside between Jasper and Cordova. Only occasionally as we tilled the soil down in the new ground would Daddy cock his head to one side, urging quietly, "Listen, listen, I b'lieve that's the 'leben o'clock passenger train pulling inta' the station right now." Then looking almost directly overhead to the sun, he'd agree with himself, "Yep, bound to be 'er." Next he'd include us in his musings, "Not more'n an hour 'fore dinner time so let's hit it like fighting fire."

Visiting at my Aunt Margaret's in the small town of Berry was a different story. The trains were close to folks and their lives down there. My aunt would fuss and fume about the ashes from the coal-burning trains settling on her just laundered sheets. My cousin knew all the trains and their schedules. When the chain on the front porch swing started rattling he'd suddenly jump up and yell, "That's the mail train from Birmingham; let's go!"

We'd run like the wind the couple of blocks to the post office, fly—just to watch the little "arm on the train" reach out and grab the mail pouch which was hanging on a high hook near the tracks.

Sometimes Jim and I'd bound down to the tracks in order to see the long freight trains come smoking and hissing through town. Go so near we'd have to plug our ears from the whistle and the clanging of the bell of the highballing freight. Stand there just to read the names Southern, Chesapeake & Ohio, or Rock Island. And to count the cars: six cattle cars with mooing cows in them, seven coal cars, the 20 box cars hiding bales of cotton and secrets inside, and the 16 flat cars—two with logs but all the others with tanks and other war equipment on them. Plus four tank cars with gas or such, which we also figured were headed off to Europe. And always there'd be the engineer in the engine and somebody in the caboose, there for no other reason—we thought—than to wave to us and other kids.

When the passenger trains pulled into Berry there'd be somebody waiting to sell parched peanuts for a nickel a bag or fresh vegetables to the train crew and interested passengers. Jim'd always just stand there, in a daze, moving his head side to side, muttering, "Boy, howdy, I'd shore like'ta ride up front on that big ole cow-catcher, jest one time in my life." But I'd beg him not to and he never did get on it.

On a few occasions while Jim and I were down by the tracks, I slipped inside the little train station and secretly dreamed of someday walking up to the window and buying a ticket, of riding one of those trains. And maybe even eating in the fancy dining room like Jim and I'd seen dressed-up folks a'doing one night. It was the night the train got derailed downtown and we stood beside the track, looking into the train windows while the folks were having their dinner served at little tables with white cloths on them, and eating outta shining dishes and using forks and knives what sparkled s'much it'd most nigh make ye go blind.

And part of my dream DID come to pass. I was almost nine. Somehow I was the lucky child out of our bunch chosen to board the train with Daddy at Berry one Saturday and ride to Kennedy. Uncle Ferman drove to meet us, taking us on to visit him and Granny

Porter. The entire cross-two-county-lines trip ate up most of a day. Yet it had taken weeks for planning, then later consumed years remembering. I just never could forget: the fancy seats, the lights overhead, nor the tall, straight conductor walking up and down, calling, "Tickets, please! Tickets, please!" And, Oh, how my heart beat fast when he came, calling, "Kennedy! Kennedy! Next stop, Kennedy!" The wonder of the day helped me to forget my disappointment over not eating in the dining car.

Recently I jumped into my Mercury sedan and drove the same distance in little more'n the time it takes to cut hot butter. There was no gentle conductor to enjoy but when I arrived my aged Uncle Ferman was still there, at the home place Daddy and I visited five decades back. My kin told me of his contribution, in the early 20s, toward building some of those railroads in rural parts of Alabama.

"It uz late summer, the fall 'fore I married. Me and Troy Anderson, and three more fellers went over there. And they's laying off men coming 'n going. I seed Mr. McConnell, the main man; I called him aside, said to 'em, "Now we come over here two weeks ago, you told us 't come back today and you'd put us on." He looked in his little book, said, "Well, I shore did." So he put us to work.

"Paid us thirty cents an hour, 'leben hours a day; three dollars and thirty cents all total. And then it cost me 'bout a dollar a day fer rations— we mostly just et salmon, biscuits, and molasses—just sorta got by on salmon, hardly ever et a chicken."

When I asked he said, "Naw, didn't have to pay fer sleeping quarters, explaining,"They'd put two boxcar houses together about a mile beyond the end of the railroad and they put a little hall about a yard wide betwixt 'em. One was the kitchen, the other the sleeping place. I'd brought my cot and I slept there. They's no screens, no doors, no nuthin' to keep the mad dogs, snakes, 'er 'sketters, er nuthing outta there. The place wad'nt much bigger'n Maw's smokehouse but we stayed.

Then one day they came by saying, "Too many men, too many men, we jest got too many men...." And they let Troy and a lotta others go but let me stay on. And soon we started in doing contract work. And they started picking buddies fer the work. I wadn't no size fer that hard work 'er hewing crossties up there 'it

Brownsville—I'se 20-year-old but didn't weigh but a hundred thirty —but I did "put on", got up to a hundred and fifty-one fore I married."

"Well, Henry Wheat called me and asked me about being his buddy. I said, 'Mr. Henry, I ain't got but one thang to do and that's go home. I ain't got no tools nor money to buy 'em.' I'd bought a T-Model car not long 'fore Margie died and I'ze making the payments on it. 'Bout $27.64 a month, I b'lieve, to be exact."

"Then Mr. Henry said, ' Well, I've got a few tools. 'Bout all we'd need!' And we went to making $5-$6 per day on the contract. But then it was gathering time and I had to come home to pick mine and Perve's cotton crop—we had it planted on the halves. I just got a fourth otta seven bales, 'sides the corn. Boss man tried his best to git me to stay on. Said I could work up to a better job—said, why didn't I jest give my crop to my Daddy. But I come on home, quit hewing them crossties 'n other thangs."

Even long ago I appreciated folks who had a hand in building the wondrous railways, even though my contact with them was skimpy. My husband, on the other hand, lived all his life where we do now, where a fast-moving train will make your rising dough fall. Where,

when I first moved into this house 17 years
ago, I awoke, petrified, at all hours of the night.
Every time a train came down the tracks I felt
like it was coming through the bedroom. Yea,
from the from the earliest age my husband has
had an intimate contact with railroads and
trains.

Joe was only four, five when he'd drive
his little goat cart—built by his grandpa—up
to the railroad. Ride up there and watch the
trains go by. Other times he and cousins Billy,
Sis, and Robert Beckham would put every
penny they could rake or scrape onto the rails.
As soon as a train had passed they'd run and
search for the flattened coins in the nearby
grass or cinders. By the time he was ten he and
the cousins rushed through chores to walk the
rails barefooted; they vied to see who could
balance and walk on a rail the farthest without
falling off. Luckily for them and their parents,
you can see trains a long way in either direction from our junction.

Joe's greatest fascination, when he was a
kid, with things associated with the railroad—
he now admits—were the hobos who jumped
off and on the trains and sometimes came to
their house. Joe recalls, "The men would al-

ways come to the back door and say, "Missus,
you got any work I could do for a bite to eat?"
He also remembers, "No matter when nor how
many stopped, Mu always managed to find
something for them to eat—leftovers, a jelly
sandwich. And sometimes she'd ask them to
chop a little stovewood; that was about all
she'd ask. She was afraid for me to be out there
around them but I'd sometimes stop and talk
to 'em."

"I'd ask their names," Joe continued,
"they called themselves things like 'Frisco Big
Man,' 'Toledo Jim,' but one was just 'Joe the
Hobo.' When I told him I was 'Joe' he started
calling me 'Little Joe the Hobo.' And he talked
about San Francisco and asked me if I'd ever
been to New York. He seemed so smart and he
made 'jumping the rails' sound like such fun.
I begged my Mama, as an eight-year-old, to let
me go with him and be a 'Little Joe the Hobo'."

"Sometimes after dark," Joe still related,
"we'd see a light in the woods, near the railroad
tracks. Down where they'd built a little camp-
fire to stay overnight. Once we even found
where they'd cooked something in a big old
can, some said it was probably 'hobo stew.' An
old feller who lived near us said hobos had

signals for each other; that they'd leave a sign for the next feller, say, that my Mu could be depended on for a good meal."

A friend told me that hobos often came to their house looking for food and a place to sleep as well. When they came saying, "Missus, know any place where I can sleep tonight?"— they were referred to the unlocked depot or the Methodist church. She remembered the hobos usually gobbled up any food given them but once her mom, thinking he needed a good diet, gave the feller —among other things —some spinach with boiled eggs on top. After the hobo had eaten and departed, her mom found the spinach piled beside the doorstep.

I read that nowadays there is a fad among yuppies of becoming hobos, bucking the system and riding the rails for recreation. I read where one such feller came to a hobo gathering on a corporate lear jet; yet he gets his kicks by occasionally jumping a freight. I can identify with them, having had a fascination with trains all my life. My husband is also in sympathy with the elite hobos; for many years he watched the rails and longed to ride them as 'Little Hobo Joe.'

Ice Cream For The Fourth:
Hand Turned In
A Syrup Bucket

The sign on the little wayside place proclaimed boldly, HAND-CHURNED ICE CREAM. I screeched to a halt and rushed in, expecting a daddy to be sitting there. Anticipating a daddy to be sitting, hunched over, turning—with hands half-frozen—a syrup pail inside a water bucket filled with ice.

Coming upon such an announcement, such an oasis, on a recent steamy day made my thoughts race backwards to a Fourth-of-July celebration in my childhood. An unusual Fourth when we lived too far away to spend the day with the kinfolks who owned ice cream freezers. Our isolation, however, turned it into a most memorable day.

During that long, hot June the endless field chores were rendered bearable by dreams of the once-a-year frozen dessert. Daddy reminded my little brother of it often as we took a breather in the shade out near the Back Forty. "Yep, Square (Squire) Skimp, I'm a'gettin' a hunderd pound block uh that ice from th' ice house in town on the 'third'. And, by jingoes, on The Fourth we're gonna have us a time, gonna freeze that cream same as if we' uz at Granny's !"

And, keeping his promise, Daddy hitched a ride into Berry with Mr. Courington that third. Went with him in the old ratt-ley pickup because he couldn't risk the ice on a long, hot wagon ride.

When they returned one dripping block of the 'semi-precious stone' was transferred quickly to our smokehouse's earthen floor. It was placed in the scratched-out cavern of the huge pile of new sawdust which had recently been hauled from the sawmill. Daddy hollered his repeated "thankee, thankee" into the dusty whirlwind behind the departing pickup as we siblings scrambled to pack the fine wooden crumbs around the ice.

Once the packing was complete, the clean

but ragged quilts were placed around the massive potential bulk, tucked as carefully as a baby being wrapped against a blizzard's breath. As we reluctantly left the ice alone, the latch on the protective door was lowered, almost ceremoniously, as hallowed against the long-awaited morrow.

The ice-cream making was begun about three o'clock, after we siblings had been on our Sunday-best behavior all day.

In the hottest part of the day Mama went into the kitchen to mix the ingredients for freezing. First she beat three fresh eggs in a bowl, then poured in a cup of sugar, beating again with the wooden spoon. To that she added a teaspoon of Watkin's vanilla flavoring. Then she skimmed and added every last drop of the cream from the milk that Bill had quickly fetched from the spring. After that was thoroughly mixed Mama took a tiny taste, smacking ever so pleasedly, and carefully poured the concoction into a gallon syrup bucket. Milk was added until the mixture reached the level of the 'eyes' into which the bucket bail was fastened. A lid was attached lastly and then it sat, waiting for Daddy to holler, "Pearlie, the ice is ready!"

Preparing the ice that day was more complicated than bursting open a plastic bag of uniformly shaped ice cubes is today. Taking a clean dishpan and his sharpened Barlow knife Daddy went to the smokehouse. The quilts were removed, the moist sawdust was raked back with his large hands, and he began to chip the precious commodity ever so gently in a line. His quick, easy picks were all monitored by the eight pairs of inquisitive eyes standing back a'ways, eyes hopeful that a stray piece of ice might fly in their direction.

Daddy's plan was to remove a generous corner from the block, chop it away without crushing it into small pieces. So after the small line was firmly entrenched around the ice Daddy drew back and made two or three hard thrusts, or stabs, if you please, into the cracks. And, right on schedule, off the large chunk broke. Bill rushed up with the dishpan, catching every last sliver.

The ice was then briefly rinsed of its sawdust, washed quickly lest the precious ice all melt. Then Daddy carefully picked the ice into pieces, carefully lest he also punch a hole into Mama's dishpan.

Mama brought the syrup bucket with its

promise inside. Frances fetched the emptied white porcelain water bucket from the back porch shelf. And, making do without ice cream salt the way we were, I totted the little white cloth bag of non-iodized salt out to the front porch, to the edge where Daddy would freeze the cream. Totted it out and made sure it didn't get near water.

Daddy placed the syrup pail in the center of the water bucket and held it firmly in place by means of its bail, or handle, extended upward. Bill scooped in ice, making sure there was a layer all around the syrup bucket. Mama took up a handful of the salt and sifted a little trail all around the bucket, over the top of the ice. Daddy turned the bucket by means of the bail, jiggled it, to make sure a large piece of ice would not prevent movement.

Another layer of ice was put in and another layer of salt. On and upward it was filled, until it almost reached the top of the pail. Daddy began turning the smaller bucket inside the larger bucket, churned it back and forth, back and forth, ever so smoothly, so gently, so rhythmically. He turned ever so patiently while we kiddoes watched and waited so impatiently.

(A friend, Garnet Stephens of Dresden, TN shared that her family inserted two "big spoons" into the syrup to jiggle around — to keep the milk stirred for more uniform freezing in the absence of a "paddle" inside the "freezer." Another lady said her family would occasionally "open up the syrup bucket and stir the cream, making sure it wouldn't become icy in spots.")

Daddy watched the improvised freezer cautiously as the ice began to melt and the water began to rise; the salty solution must be poured off carefully before it reached the "eyes" lest it seep through into the freezing cream.

We each clamored for, and were given, a chance to turn the bucket. As the cream hardened, however, turning it became more and more difficult, even with a padding of old paper around the freezing-cold wire bail. Soon Daddy announced, "It's finished!" amid shouts all around. Then he added, "But it'll be better if we let it set awhile." So paper was spread over the top and an extra padding of a burlap bag was added for the wait. Meanwhile we rushed to assemble tin spoons and chipped cups and bowls for the magical moment.

Soon the padding was removed, the syrup

pail lifted out and the lid pried off. Mama
dished up the white mountains of ice cream
and we sat around the porch— licking, smacking, slowly relishing the delicious taste that
was so rare, so special. Such a heavenly treat
on a sweltering hot day long ago drew our
family so close.

The recent sign, HAND-CHURNED ICE
CREAM, sent me racing inside the shop, expecting to see a daddy sitting there, churning
a syrup pail back and forth. Primed my taste
buds for ice cream like we enjoyed on a long-
ago Fourth of July. I guess it's no wonder I was
so disappointed, so downcast when I entered
the store and saw only an electric cord pro-
truding from a fancy ice-cream freezer, and
there was no Daddy nor family around.

MAMA'S HOMEMADE VANILLA ICE CREAM

(For one gallon, which is more than a syrup
bucket held.)

4 Fresh Hen Eggs   1 1/2 C sugar
2 tsp Watkins Vanilla
3 qts cream and top milk
Crushed ice   Non-iodized salt or Rock Salt

Mix as in foregoing story. Fill freezer to

fill line, or about three-fourths full. Freeze until hard to turn handle. Cover and let set about 15-20 minutes. Deeeeliciouuuuss!

"COOKED" HOMEMADE ICE CREAM
Elsie Neal, Williston, FL

Elsie says that as a child her family would go by the ice house most Sundays, after church, and buy 50 pounds of ice. They would make a gallon of ice cream for dinner, a gallon for supper, using the good milk and eggs their animals produced. Elsie still uses her Mom's recipe, following:

2 C sugar   4 eggs, beaten
1/4 C flour   1 C cream (or 1 can evap. milk)
1/2 gal of milk (or enough to fill the churn)
1 tsp vanilla

In heavy saucepan put 2 C of milk, on medium heat. Mix sugar and flour together and stir into the milk. Beat the eggs, add a little milk, and next add this mixture to the heated milk, stirring until the entire mixture becomes thickened a little and the eggs are thoroughly cooked. Cool, add vanilla and cream, pour into ice cream churn. Add sufficient milk to fill the container. Freeze. (Two cups of sweetened fruit—such as peaches or

pineapple—may be added before freezing.)
***FAYE'S NOTE: We did not hurry to dispose
of the salty water and leftover ice from the
water bucket long ago. Instead, every smidgen
bit was utilized, saved. Right off the bat Bill
would "double dog dare" me to get a handful of
the ice, add a generous amount of salt, and run
around the house a couple of times, squeezing
it real hard. The first time I took the dare I
ended up with a blister inside my hand, I did.

Then we danced around, still giddy from
the joy of the ice cream, grabbing bits of ice
and putting it down each other's shirts and
blouses. This was not a trick nor treatment, as
it's considered today. Those days of hot weather
without fans and air-conditioning, we considered it a real treat to have ice put down one's
back.

Mama would not let us waste very much
of the leftover ice, however, on excited fun. The
small pieces were rinsed of their salty water at
the edge of the yard, using water from the well.
And they were re-cycled. They provided us
with a second treat for the day: iced tea for
supper. You see, Mama had bought a one-
pound box of "loose tea grounds" from the
Watkins Man for the Fourth. She made the tea

in a little boiler on the woodstove, then strained it through a sleazy (thin) flour sack. While the discarded leaves became fertilizer for Mama's potted plants which were growing in leaky chamber pots on the front porch edge—well, the leaves served their purpose after the strength was drawn from them to make a delicious drink for our Fourth of July supper. Or, if we didn't have tea we would have milk for supper, just-milked milk which was cooled down with the remnants of ice from the ice cream freezer. Talk about mileage — we really got lots of mileage from a hundred pounds of ice long ago!

Grandma's Old Gray Goose: The Wedding Feast

I read in the papers of couples who tie the knot in mid-air after both them and the minister have parachuted out of a plane, of twosomes who jump the broom out on the lake on waterskiis, and of others being joined as one while wearing oxygen tanks, submerged beneath the ocean. Even my eldest son, Greg, pledged Delores to "love and cherish you forever" in a small ceremony on top of an ancient Indian temple mound, under the glow of a full autumn moon. And church weddings are, frequently, the culmination of months of planning and the spending of untold thousands in cash. But the tragedy of it all is that so many of the unique weddings don't last. It's as if, too often now-a-days, the CEREMONY becomes the focal point for the couple and after the exciting extravanganza is over it's all down hill from there.

It is not my intent to imply that young men and women didn't resort to unusual tactics and schemes to get hitched long ago; they did. My Uncle Ferman drove by school early one morning and picked up Gertrude; they lit out as fast as that Ford car would go, straight to the courthouse. And right on their tail, driving mad and feverishly after hearing of the unapproved scheme, was Gertrude's father.

One day long ago my future mother-in-law quietly donned her mother's new dress and went for a ride with her heartthrob, Ralph. Joining them for the short trip into Tuscaloosa was her sister Pauline and her husband James. After parking, one of the men summoned Reverend Marler from the nearby store where he worked. He, in turn, stood beside the car while the seated couple pledged their vows. Ralph then returned to his folks' home: Elizabeth went back to hers. Early next morning Elizabeth's widowed Mom high-tailed it to town and back, sacrifically presenting her daughter with a new dress for the wedding she had a hunch was soon upcoming. Elizabeth then broke down and admitted she was already 'Mrs. Ralph Brown' ; she subsequently moved into that role.

Bill and Erma went one night to the minister's house. He came in from his farm chores, wearing dirty overalls. He agreed to tie the knot but excused himself and put on his black preacher suit first.

Cuple and her "TO-BE" did involve family and friends in their "elaborate" wedding plans. Her Papa took her into town for a new dress, then he headed back to the fields. She donned the dress and together the couple, plus several of their young friends, walked up to the mail-box. They flagged down the letter-carryin' preacherman. He parked his car then walked a'ways with 'em, assembled 'em on a bridge— where the two then "took the plunge." The new couple next enjoyed the lunch her mama had stayed behind to prepare, and headed out walking the short distance to the groom's family's home. There they spent their "honey-moon" and their early married years.

My heart recalls a wedding ceremony in the early 50s. My older sister, Frances, with whom I had always shared a room and the

secrets of my life, was marrying her high school
sweetheart in May, just after her graduation.
As the days drew nearer and nearer for her
"departure from my life," I cherished the minutes we sat on the edge of our bed, talking of
her venture, inhaling deeply of the intoxicat-
ing sweetness which wafted each spring from
the beautiful gardenia bush just outside our
opened windows. And we chatted as she twirled,
excitedly, before the chifferobe mirror. Model-
ing the stylish platform 4-inch-heels and the
beautiful white satin ballerina-length wedding
dress which Mama had lovingly fashioned with
fabric from the catalog.

Even in her happiness my sister lan-
guished a bit over forfeiting her long-standing
dream to be married in a "Gardenia-Bush-
Wedding." Over failure to say "I DO" in our
yard with its waiting bridal arch carved into
the hedge and the gardenia bush perfuming
the air as the sun slowly sank.

But because there was so little money
Frances, instead, wore a symbolic corsage of
the gardenias and she and Douglas rode away
on a hot Saturday afternoon into town. There—
in the Methodist parsonage—in the presence
of the minister's wife, Douglas's sister Ruth,

and myself, plus two ruffians—our brother Bill and his friend Tim who rushed down, uninvited, from the picture show—there, before the six of us, the friend Frances and Douglas had learned to love and trust from high school chapel sermons quickly blessed their union.

Yes, the pledging of wedding vows in the presence of God seemed to carry more weight than the trappings of a fancy or unique ceremony long ago. And many of the girls and boys, like my sister Frances, chose to cut a few corners off the edges of their dreams in order to have more time with the one they loved. If Gertrude's dad had arrived ten minutes earlier, before their final "I DO," she and Ferman would probably never have celebrated 66 years of a wonderful married partnership in 1993. If Bill and Erma had waited for an elaborate church wedding they would no doubt not have had many happy years before Bill's death. If Elizabeth had waited for a fine trouseau she'd have passed over four decades with Ralph. Cuple opted for the "now almost six decades" of weathering life's storms with her faithful hubby rather than hang around hoping for a prince to take her immediately to a fine castle.

But, then again, some weddings long ago

did involved the extended families more than the above mentioned ones. Take, for instance, Buna's wedding and the subsequent happenings. She, her hubby-to-be, plus his uncle and aunt, rode together in a buggy one rainy, rainy night to the parson's house. According to her, "Well, it wudn't no big t'do. After we were jined, we come back home to eat supper and spend the night. No, Mama didn't go to the wedding; she stayed home and cooked. Well, atter supper the uncle and others started playing checkers. And they played checkers, and had a gay old time, and jest kept playing checkers...bad thang about it was—they's in the room with us, in the room where we's gonna sleep. Didn't matter to them, though, they jest stayed on til atter midnight."

And there was my Uncle Vic's wedding feast in '41, when Grandma Shirley cooked her old grey goose. Well, their ceremony down at the courthouse was just a tip o' th' iceberg, too, compared to the party afterwards. Well, I don't mean there was drinking 'er carousing, or nothing like that; the Fess Shirley's, my Mama's folks, well they's all Christians and didn't b'lieve in drinking a drop but they did like't git together whenever they could—and have a good time. So when the only boy of the bunch announced he's a'marrying Amy, well, they started in a'writing letters 'n planning a big blowout.

Mama got Uncle Bud to come the twenty-odd miles in his car and take us to her Mama and Papa's. That 'uz three grown-ups and six younguns in, and on, that little old car. I remember sitting in the rumble seat with Daddy, and Bill, and some uv my sisters—going over, and under, the tall metal frame-work of Shirley Bridge down in Sipsey swamp, and the awe of it as dusky dark was comin' on. (It loomed as imposing to me, back then, as the Eiffel Tower in Paris now does.)

When we got to Grandma's up near Brownsville, WOOOooooeeeee—everything was smelling better'n Christmas. Grandma had killed, picked, and cooked her special, giant-sized old grey goose. Ohhhhhh, and she had all the trimmings—dressing, and yams, and rolls...plus some of the girls had baked up a big coconut cake for the wedding.

Earl and Jessie and their two boys uz there; Margaret and Doc and Troy; Bud and Bert and Mackey; and Zula with Therman and their three boys. And, of course the honorees!

Wow, what a passel of folks, especially uv younguns and crying babies. But mostly everybody was hugging Vic and Amy, and welcoming her to the family and everybody was talking and laughing all at the same time.

We ate at first tables, and second tables, and third tables and still they'uz plenty of that giant old goose and the dressing with 'im. Grandpa and Uncle Vic wuz teasing back and forth with Grandma; they knew she'd been partial to the old bird and sorta hated to get rid of 'im, even if he wad'nt no 'count. And I 'spected Grandpa uz trying t'keep from being so sad about his only son marrying and leaving.

Said Grandpa, "Well, they say ye can't slip daylight past a rooster, but I got one up on that. Ye couldn't slip it past Nancy's old grey goose either. He'd be up a'squawking and a'squealing to beat the mischief ever mornin' jest't th' break o'day; if a'body ever got a chance to lie a'bed t'wouldn't do no good, couldn't sleep fer that bird a hollering. Anythang worse'n a no-good-rooster 'r a crowin' hen is a crowin' goose!"

Uncle Vic laughed, slapped his knee, and said, "Yea, too bad I won't be here now t'enjoy

th'peace with ye, Poppa." Everybody jest
hollered, including my Grandma Nancy.

Then it 'uz Grandma's turn. She started
talking about all the wonderful "down" that
wuz on that big goose, said 'spect it'd be most
nigh enough to make a "down piller," atter it
wuz aired and dried and sunned for weeks.
Hearing that, Uncle Vic and Grandpa changed
their tune, both started in a 'begging to be the
one to have the piller, said they's s'much
finer'n a hen-feather piller.

We all had a grand time at the wedding
feast; with a start on marriage like that, and all
the family pulling for 'em, it's no wonder the
couple's passed their Golden Wedding Anni-
versary, still in love.

I will have to admit though, there WERE
a few instances back then when everything in
a marriage just went haywire. Like Ruby shared
with me about her folks. Said she was about
five when her daddy strayed to a bootlegger's
abode for a little fun. Her fiery mama drove the
old Model-T touring car down there, with her
and her eleven-year-old sister sitting in the
rear. Well, her Mama stopped the Tin Lizzie,
left the motor running and ran inside the
"tavern." According to Ruby her mama must've

caused a "hellacious ruckus" cause in no time both mama and daddy came runnin' out the door, jumped into the idling car, and flew outta there at top speed—35 mph—like a giant bird! Right behind them, puffing out the door, came the genteel pro-pri-e-ter with a 410 double barrel shotgun and fired at the rear of Lizzie. Ruby said "Only thing between us and that buckshot was Almighty God and thin tin; if mama hadn't left the motor running, and the Good Lord hadn't been with us, my sis and I would've only been two left-over greasy spots!"

I recently read where a peniless couple was determined to have a fancy wedding, re-gardless. So they engaged in a wedding-day-shoplifting-spree. Went everywhere stealing everything—a $500 wedding gown, a veil, suits for the groom and attendants, even camera and film and two cushions for the ring bearer. They, like many other couples with today's "marrying 'n leaving" philosophy, forgot the real thing of importance about getting married; they put the emphasis on the social part of the ceremony.

We need to get back, like long ago, when just the taking of the vows was the important door through which couples who loved each other entered into sharing life. Entered into taking the good and the bad together. Like some of them settin' up housekeeping with little more'n a 25-piece set of dishes, and a five-piece aluminum cooking set, which had been earned by selling a total of thirty-two jars of Rosebud Salve for twenty-five cents each. Then later facing the odds that my great-grandma did—she and her husband losing four babies on the same day, dead of colitis. But they stuck it out and faced it together. Like one old-timer said to me, "Chile, when some troubles come up'un ye, all ye can do is 'bear 'em; bear 'em together, Chile, bear 'em with yo man by yo side."

The Saga Of The Sage Brush:
From Broom To Cake Tester

Fields which have lain fallow in my neck of the woods are now laden with ripened broom straw (or broomsedge), acres and acres of the orange sage brush just swaying in the fall breeze. Whispering through the wind, begging me and other housewives to hurry. To partake freely of the bounty before the winter rains turn its golden orange heads into rotted, dark, and useless stubble.

The gentle call of the unmade sage brush brooms, ours for the taking, goes unanswered, however. I and others like me whiz past, casting only admiring glances. We're off to Walmart or Service Merchandise, spending good money for an O'Cedar light and easy cornbroom, or even worse, an electric vacuum-sweeper.

Such was not the case when I was young; all the households with which I had contact as a child relied heavily on sage brush brooms. Come fall the sight of a field swaying heavily with the straw was considered a blessing from God, brooms aplenty for an entire year.

Every year, on one bright October Saturday, after harvesting of the cotton and corn was completed, Mama always awakened us with, "Up and at it, you sleepy heads, it's Sage Brush Broom Day!" By the time we had eaten a hearty breakfast and dressed she'd say, "Speck the dew's 'bout dried off. Bill, you harness up old Maude and hitch her to the ground slide while the girls wash up the dishes. I'll sharpen up the butcher knives, then we'll be off."

It was a happy troupe that made it's way to the spied-out "fine patch of sage brush." Three or four of the younger kids hitched a ride on the slide, squealing and hanging on for dear life when Bill detoured over the cotton patch with its emptied rows and terraces turning the ride into a roller-coaster one.

Many folks in our neighborhood insisted on "wringing" the straw for their brooms; grabbing a wad of it in their hand and twisting 'round and 'round until it broke. Our Mama— thank the Good Lord— was sympathetic with our complaints that doing so resulted in cuts and tears to our hands. She therefore used, and permitted us older siblings to also employ, butcher knives to slash handfuls of the straw from its roots.

The younger kiddoes sometimes helped secure big bundles of the potential brooms with twine and tote them back to the waiting slide. Most often, however, they crawled around in the fluffy straw, once laughing, yelling, then quietly sneaking up on each other, hollering, "Grrrrr, gotcha." They were exhausted— and covered with beggar-lice— for the long walk home when the sage brush claimed their spaces on the ground slide. Only the tiniest tot was permitted to sleep on the fuzzy ends as we headed to the barn to store the straw.

Gathering and storing sage brush was only the embryo stage in the life of our brooms. Assisting in the birth of a broom consisted of being sent, one day, to the loft for a large wad of the straw. Then outside, in the blowing wind, the cord was cut—so to speak— by putting a butcher knife to use once again. Up and down, over and under, in and out of the straws one sliced. Cutting away the outsides, the peelings, the husks from the straws' bodies, if you please. Paring them down to the nubs.

Tying of the straws was an important last step in a broom's beginning. Once a just-right handful of straws was readied the winding and securing began. Most often at our house it was done by means of twine saved from the guano sacks. Exciting indeed was the acquisition of a "rubber band" for the purpose; a strip of rubber cut from an old inner tube a neighbor had discarded. Either medium required skill and firmness; the straws had to be secured tightly for its many uses.

Lastly, the finished broom's head was beaten, or thrashed, against the side of the corncrib or smokehouse. This caused the extra fuzz and the seeds of the fluffy sage brush to fly away in the wind before being taken inside for sweeping the house. If a floor was swept without completing this final step it resulted in fuzz flying all over the house, creating more debris than the sweeping eliminated.

Brooms in all stages of their childhood and adult lives could be found around our rooms, our porches, our buildings long ago. The newest, freshly-made brooms were taken to the front room, the room where Mama and Daddy slept, where the family sat around the fireplace every night, doing lessons, shelling a bushel of corn for the grist mill, or sometimes shelling a few ears of popcorn for popping.

At bedtime the new broom was grabbed to "sweep up a bit" before heading to bed. Care had to be taken while sweeping the stray ashes into the fireplace, care that the tips of the straw did not catch fire and burn the good broom. (We kids had to scamper during the sweeping; otherwise someone would sweep under our feet, this meant we'd never get to marry.)

After sweeping, the new broom took its place, standing near the fireplace, fluffy end up. From there it was retrieved early every morning by Mama or a teenaged daughter; the entire house was swept thoroughly with it. The long, limber broom was especially good for reaching under beds, into corners, for sweeping cobwebs from the ceilings.

The sage brush brooms were also great for mixing a little fun with the work. Even my busy Mama could be seen taking time from the sweeping to tease the kitten. Be caught permitting Midnight to pounce for the extended broom, drawing it back quickly—back and forth, having a time of play.

Today's cake recipes dictate "insert cake tester" to determine if a cake is baked sufficiently. We did not have a store-bought cake tester when I was a young girl. Instead, I will—shamefacedly—admit to you that we used a broom straw for that purpose. When we opened the door of the old wood stove's oven and saw that the everyday cake was browning we ran for the newest broom. Pulled a single straw upwards from the handle end and broke off a small piece to insert into the cake. If no batter adhered to the straw the cake was removed from the oven, was done. (It now seems the straw was a better indictor than all the cake testers and oven thermometers available today.)

We took straws randomly from our brooms for other purposes as well. We jerked them out to pick our teeth with. And many a night after supper Mama pulled a broom straw, broke it into four pieces of varying lengths and lined the pieces up between her pinched fingers. With the extended lengths even and the uneven ends hidden, she let us "draw straws " to settled arguments. The one who got the longest straw had to wash the dishes, the next longest dried them. The recipient of the third one put them away, and the shortest straw meant you took care of the baby for awhile.

Brooms which had seen better days, which no longer had limber, slender straws were still useful around our home. They were assigned to stand like sentinels on our porches. From there they were snatched up quickly to get the old Tom cat out of the kitchen and head him to the barn for the night. Or to chase dogs off the porch. The instrument could also be used to run a stray banty rooster from the porch or steps.

An old, almost-had-it sage brush broom might be found in our crib years ago. There it came in handy to sweep out a spot to sit and shell a bushel of corn. Or you could use the compact piece of equipment to throw at a wharf rat that dared show it's tail around the corner. We often relegated such a broom to our out-house, our toilet. It was handy to keep it swept with, or to throw at a snake that came slithering from underneath the Sears-Roebuck cattylog —if anyone remained in the toilet long enough to throw under such circumstances.

Mama tried her hand one year at growing some broom corn. Had pretty good luck. The brooms she fashioned with the corn by tying the straw onto an old hoe handle—well, they were rather nice. Lasted much, much longer than the sage brush brooms we made and didn't put out nearly as much fuzz when new. But somehow it was just not the same; we missed our handy, lightweight brooms. And so the next year we made sure we didn't miss a chance on a bright October day to sashay over to the field and cut down enough broom straw for a year's worth of brooms.

Today, half-a-century later I watch from my kitchen window the field of gently swaying orange-topped broom straw, whispering for me to hurry before the winter rains begin. Reason tells me I have cleaning items a-plenty on hand; dust mops, O'Cedar cornbrooms, and my electric sweeper. But memory has the upper hand. So excuse me, I'm heading out the door with my butcher knife. Besides, a light-weight sage brush broom will be easier on my aging back; it'll sure be quieter than the sweeper when I'm tending my grand-niece, Rebecca; and I'll have plenty of cake testers on hand for baking the goodies in this GRANNY'S TEACAKES... book.

A Miracle: Sorghum 'Lasses Into Gingerbread

Gingerbread was a delicious 'standby' dessert when I was growing up. Mama made it often, especially during the WW II days when sugar was rationed. Early in my life I came to equate gingerbread with 'shortening bread' and every time Mama went into the kitchen to stir up some gingerbread all of us youngun's would gather 'round, begging to help crack the eggs, and do the stirring. Then we'd begin to sing, to the top of our lungs, the following old folk song:

> *"Mama's little baby loves shawt'nen',*
>   *shawt'nen',*
> *Mama's little baby loves shawt'nen'*
>   *bread.*
> *Slipp't in de kitchen, slipp't up de lid,*
> *Slipp't my pockets full o' shawt'nen'*
>   *bread.*
> *Stole de skillet, stole de lid,*
> *Stole dat gal makin' shawt'nen' bread.*

Mama's little baby loves shawt'nen',
   shawt'nen',
Mama's little baby loves shawt'nen' bread!

The way we jumped around and kept singing, and singing, and acting out the song—it was a "Pure miracle from God," Mama said, "that th' gingerbread rose at all; the way you younguns' jarred that old wood stove."

The gingerbread we enjoyed cooking most of all was the cookie dough Mama let us transform into gingerbread men. We had no cutter so we either put a cardboard pattern onto the rolled out, stiff dough and cut around it—ever so slowly, carefully—or we made originals, each kid in the bunch just rolling out a wad of dough and carving their unique gingerbread man.

Some of the men evolved from the case knives looking skinny as a rail, others emerged fat and wobbly. But almost all came from the oven with shiny eyes and buttons made of raisins or hikker nut pieces. The precious cookies were never eaten without the reciting, and movements of the Gingerbread Man story, over and over—until finally when the gingerbread men could no longer run from the little old woman and the little old man... until one by one they stepped onto the fox's nose and "SNAP," one of the Porter kids took a huge, delicious bite of the fun fellow.

Following are several wonderful variations of gingerbread:

GINGERBREAD MEN

1/2 C softened butter	*1/2 C sugar*
1/2 C sorghum syrup	*1 beaten egg*
1/2 tsp baking soda	*3 1/2 C flour*
1/2 tsp ginger	*1/4 tsp salt*

Cream butter and sugar, add syrup and egg. Combine all dry ingredients and add gradually to the first mixture. Mix well. If too stiff, add 2-4 T of water to manage. Roll out on flour surface and cut the gingerbread men. Transfer to greased cookie sheet—carefully—to avoid breaking any legs or arms. Decorate as desired. Bake at 375 degrees for 12-15 minutes. Makes about 10-12 gingerbread men. (Don't forget to sing, recite the story, and eat the leftover dough.)

MOLASSES TEACAKES

Patsy Morgan, Scottsville, KY from
Patsy's great-grandmother, Patsy Ann Weaver

Patsy says she still makes these often, as did her grandmother, Lottie Conner.

3 1/2 C sifted plain flour   1/2 C white sugar

2 tsp baking soda   2 tsp ground cinnamon

1 tsp ground ginger   1 egg

1 C molasses   1/3 C boiling water

1/2 C shortening   1 T vinegar

Sift together flour, sugar, soda and spices. Add shortening, egg, molasses, water and vinegar. Stir together to produce a thick batter. Drop by tablespoons onto a greased cookie sheet. Bake 10-12 minutes at 375 degrees. Makes about 30 cookies.

GINGERBREAD

(In family over 100 years)

Almeda Dorrah, Coker, AL

(This can successfully be mixed with an electric mixer.)

1/2 C butter and lard, mixed   1 egg

1/2 C sugar   1 C molasses

1 1/2 tsp soda   1 tsp cinnamon

2 1/2 C flour   1 tsp ginger

1 tsp cloves   1/2 tsp salt

1 C hot water

Cream shortening and sugar. Add beaten egg and molasses, stir. Add dry ingredients which have been sifted together. Add hot water and beat until smooth. Bake in a shallow loaf pan (13 x 9 x 2) for about 40-45 minutes. Use a clean broom straw to test for doneness; if no sticky-looking cake is on the straw, it is ready. Yields 15 servings.

SOFT GINGERBREAD

Submitted by Helen Ray, Brush Creek, TN
Known as "Black George," over 70 years old,
originally from Etta Ailen

Beat one egg lightly in a cup with a fork. Add one tablespoonful melted butter, three tablespoonfuls sour milk then finish filling the cup with molasses. Turn all into a bowl and beat hard.

Add: *1 C sifted flour*   *1 tsp soda*
1 tsp cinnamon   *1 tsp cloves*
1 tsp allspice

Combine all thoroughly. Pour into greased and floured pan. Bake at 350 degrees for 30-35 minutes. When it is cool frost as below.

FROSTING:
1/2 C water   *1 C sugar*

Boil the water and sugar until it will make a "thread." Beat the white of one egg. Pour the hot syrup over the egg white and beat until it is cool. Spread over the cooled gingerbread.

Please Turn My Apple-A-Day Into Apple Butter

If my Mama had coined the phrase "An apple a day..." she'd have ended it with "...in one form or another." She missed few days of any year when her family wasn't eating apples—fresh ones, canned, dried, stewed, baked, as apple dumplings, apple sauce, apple juice, apple cobblers, jelly rolls, plate pies, fried apple pies, apple butter... always "an apple a day in one form or another."

We were blessed (or cursed, depending on whose view you took) because most yards of the tenant houses where we moved from year-to-year boasted of fine old apple trees which brought forth abundantly. And wherever there were no fruit trees upon our arrival, my Johnny-Appleseed-Daddy saw to it that there were some planted before we moved away. For my Daddy, Ira, walked hundreds of miles every summer after crop-laying-by time. Walked, selling Stark Bros. fruit trees to country and town folk alike. And all trees from the unclaimed shipments were planted near our yards.

Oh, I enjoyed having apple trees nearby where you could grab an apple occasionally to chew on. And I didn't mind picking a peck now and then for canning or turning into a delectable dish. But the thorn in my flesh was when neighbors rode by in their wagons, hollering to Mama, "They's apples jest a'wastin' up at our place; come on up and help yo' self." That was tantamount to waving a red flag in the face of a raging bull.

Before the sun had set Mama'd send me and Bill, on the ground slide, with instructions to "bring back every peeling, core, or seed they don't want." More times than not there were hundreds of rottening apples laying on the ground in these unwanted orchards. Decaying fruits which were homes for thousands of insects. Why, I am here today a miracle of the Lord, having survived the stings of a zillion bees, hornets, wasps, and yellow jackets which didn't wish to be disturbed.

Yep, having an apple-a-day in their varied forms spelled plenty of work when I was a child—work for their gathering and also work for their preservation. From the earliest apples in May until the last ones in late October we were kept busy, testimony to the fact that not an apple fell that Mama didn't mark it's fall.

When summer's days were the longest and the hottest we dried fruit. The apples we peeled; the peaches, not. But always we cored— or removed the seeds— then sliced into thin slivers. They were put outside a'mornin', after the dew dried off—spread on a thoroughly scrubbed piece of tin, placed out of reach of dogs.

And after I once balanced the sliced fruit on the woodpile only to have a young bull yearling, staked nearby, stretch his rope and eat most of the drying apples—well, after that the apples were put atop a high shed and covered over with a few yards of cheese cloth that had been ordered from the cattylog for the very purpose of keeping flies, bees, and bumblebees from our drying fruit.

It became my job to climb up and spread the fruit atop the building nearest to the heavens. The entire brood kept a vigil on the weather; if someone saw a cloud the size of a man's hand appear on the most distant horizon even the tiniest tots ran into the house calling, "Mama! Mama! the apples, the apples!" And quickly I'd scamper up and bring down the apples. Then ten minutes later the sun would come out and Mama'd holler, "Nonie Faye, the sun is out; take out the apples!" All day long it was just taking out, and bringing in, the apples... why I was skinny as a rail until I was grown, just bringing in and taking out the apples!

Yep, the situation was critical on hot summer afternoons when showers kept threatening to wet the precious fruit. It was dire enough the 3, 4, 5 days when the fruit was "on the tin." But talk about an emergency! Just let a shower threaten once you had the fruit into sacks—when bushels upon bushels of apples had been dried—patiently dried and reduced to mere tads in the bottoms of clean guano sacks. Dried but still occasionally tossed atop the roof for 'extra' sun —insurance against winter infestation of half-dried fruit by worms.

I didn't mind scrambling to save the dried fruit because come cold nights it was hard to tell which we enjoyed most—feasting on Mama's dried-apple-fried pies or having her copy Aunt Beck Hannah's "stacked dried apple cake", the one where our Great Aunt Beck patted little wads of 'teacake batter' into her 'baker' or iron griddle to cook up many layers for stacking.

Nothing from the apples was ever wasted at our house. Peelings and cores from the apples that were to be dried, turned into applesauce, or from those that were just cut into chunks and canned—every smidgen bit of everything was saved. These "trimmings" were simmered in a little water and then strained to make apple juice for later turning into jelly. Or it was just canned up as plain "apple cider" for drinking in the winter when fresh fruit was unobtainable and we were sick and needing vitamins.

Yep, it's true — I'm crazy about many apple dishes. But my absolute favorite is apple butter. I always looked forward to the time when our tart apples were ready for making the delicious sauce. "You never used sweet apples, but tart. However, they needed to be ripe, and soft, for the best results," I remember. After they were peeled and cut up, a little water was added. They were cooked in the biggest stove pot we had—cooked until they were squishy. Then Mama...or someone with a long, protecting arm—an adult—mashed them with a potato masher. It was a dangerous job—that of keeping the bubbling, threatening volcano of molten lava (the hot apple sauce) stirred to prevent sticking. Mama added sugar to the mixture at about the rate of one cup to each two cups of the apple sauce—sometimes more, depending on the taste test. Later she added ground cinnamon to taste. After two, three hours of very slow simmering, the golden brown delicacy would be ready to spread onto a buttered biscuit—or to spoon into jars for sealing for the winter. Or to take a large bowl of it and a spoon and sit under the shade tree, to relish it slowly, let the heavenly food glide gently over my tongue and down—down to tickle my inside tummy! THAT was Utopia!

Once when we were making our apple butter on the stovetop our neighbor Matilda dropped by. She told a wonderful story about visiting her aunt, as a child. While there in the mountains of Tennessee she saw them making apple butter outside, over an open fire. It was cooked, according to our friend, in a large copper kettle. She said they peeled three bushels of Winesap apples each time they made a "stir." And to keep the applebutter from popping onto the person stirring, a long-handled wooden "stirer" was used. She described it as a long pole with a "paddle" attached. The paddle had round holes bored through it. "And, truth, so help me God," Matilda said, "they cooked it all day long. And near the end they added some oil of cinnamon. After it was finished they put it into crocks, covered it with cloths, and lastly, sealed it by pouring hot paraffin over the tops."

After hearing this great story I had a recurring dream for weeks—and sometimes even yet it pops into my subconscious sleep. Seems I'd died and gone on to Heaven. God and all his angels—plus millions of other folk—were gathered outside, under giant oak trees and a beautiful blue sky. The time was early fall and hundreds of copper and brass pots sat on legs, with a tensy fire around each. And overseeing each shiny pot full of apple butter was an angel in shining apparel, hovering over, making sure that the one pulling and pushing the stirer back and forth never faltered, never let the gallons and gallons of bubbling apple butter stick to the containers and scorch.

And there were rows and rows of mamas, all rolling out, baking, and buttering biscuits with fresh butter that all the grannies were churning. And one was permitted to eat endlessly of the delicious apple butter and biscuits—and they never felt stuffed. HOLEY MOLEY, CAPTAIN MARVEL, who could ask for a better dream?

And even when I awakened as a child I was still happy. I felt comfort in knowing that I had a Johnny-Appleseed-Daddy and a Mama whose watchword was, "An Apple-a-Day...in some form or another." And that Mama very often turned my apple into apple butter.

Helen White of Lenoir City, TN recently shared with me that the tradition of making apple butter yearly in a large kettle has continued through five generations of her family. And still, once a year, the extended family gathers from around the globe for "Apple Butter Day." The excitement begins early and lasts late, young and old alike helping with peeling, mixing, and especially stirring. The boiling brass kettle (which, long ago, was a wedding present to Helen's mother-in-law from the bride's parents) has to be watched and stirred for hours. Two clean pennies are also added to the pot; the two who get the pennies in their serving of apple butter are assured of good luck to come.)

As the simmering butter nears completion a periodic check is made. A small amount of the butter is dipped into a saucer, cooled a bit, and then a "road" is made in the butter with the tester's fingertip. When the road stays clear of water—HOORAY! The apple butter is done! It is time for hot, buttered biscuits and fresh apple butter for everyone.

The Recipe:

4 bushels of apples, peeled, cored, and chopped
30 lbs sugar

Cook 5-8 hours. Yield 92 pints apple butter.

MY SISTER BETTY'S APPLE BUTTER

Betty Christian, Northport, AL

(I look forward to receiving a jar of this each Christmas.)

20 lbs tart apples   *4 C sugar*
1 T cinnamon   *1 qt. apple cider or water*

Peel, core, and chop the apples into a large soup kettle for cooking atop the stove.

Add 1 quart water or apple cider to keep from sticking until they begin to make their own juice. Cook, covered, over very low heat. When apples are tender, pulverize with potato masher. Add sugar and cinnamon. Remove lid and simmer, stirring often. When very thick and all water evaporated, spoon into hot, scalded jars and seal. Approx. 6 pints.

EASY APPLE BUTTER
Ada Smith, Madison, Indiana

13 C plain apple sauce   9 C sugar
1 C Red Hots

Bring to boil 4-5 minutes, stirring until thick enough. Spoon into hot jars, seal.

The Passing Of
The Porch Sitters
or Out Where Granny Served
Teacakes To The Heathen

I recently accompanied my salesman-husband on one of his regular road trips. Traversing the peaceful countryside, he maneuvered around sharp curves and steep hillsides that warm spring morning. Suddenly he slammed on brakes, exclaiming, directing my attention toward an aged farm house. "She's not there!" To himself as much as to me, he went on, pouring out, "A little old lady always sits on that front porch, unless it's freezing weather. Sits there and rocks in that chair and waves at me. Has for years— until today, that is." I could see the sadness gathered in his face, accepting the reality of the passing, the loss of the last of the porch sitters.

Webster defines "porch" as a covered entrance to a building. In today's world they are often just that, no more. Just a place to stand and avoid getting soaked while unlocking a door during a gully-washer. When I was a child porches were different, they had character. They were almost as important a part of the house as the kitchen or the bedroom; I can't recall even the simplest, most humble Southern home back then which had none. Most had two: a front porch and a back porch. And a few eloquent, rich-folks-houses—scattered here and there—had real fancy porches, porches that went all the way around the houses and back again. Yet even then porches were as different as the people who used them. And as I think back on porches in my past it's by how folks used 'em that I still know 'em.

The porches which intrigued me most as a child but which I seldom saw—and then only from afar—were those which surrounded huge, white antebellum homes. Once I went with a friend to deliver milk and butter to the back door of one such place. While there we heard the lady of the house inviting a spiffily-dressed caller to, "Come and sit on the verandah; I'll have Mary serve tea." As we walked away I saw them relaxing on the long porch in fancy rocking chairs, cooling themselves with palm-leaf fans, items I'd seen only in the Sears 'n Roebuck Wish Book. I looked back, longingly, dreaming of one day climbing those outside stairs to the second floor and then sliding down the curving, polished bannister until I reached the ground with a THUD.

Summers of my childhood I was always thrilled to spend a few days with my Aunt Margaret. She and her family lived in a painted house near many neighbors in a small Southern town. Their house boasted a front porch which extended very closely to the quiet, tree-lined, paved street where her neighbors strolled up and down after supper on long, hot evenings. Whenever my aunt's family and I sat on the porch, the passing folks always pulled themselves over to the edge of the street and visited a spell. They'd ask Uncle Doc if he'd heard the latest news of The War, and about how the logging was going. And he'd tell 'em, "My 'hands' 'er cuttin' some uf the biggest hardwoods up in the hills I've ever seen, but th' rattlesnakes and the heat 're almost more'n we can take."

Aunt Margaret'd volunteer that her cow—the one she kept out back in the little stall and a tiny grazing area—well, she had gone dry, was expected to calve any day. And if a car happened to creep down the street, they'd all turn their attention to it, puzzled to death if they didn't recognize the vehicle nor its occupants. And if they realized it was, "The Simpsons from up the road a'piece," they wondered aloud, "Reckon where on earth they're goin' this time o' day!"

My brother Bill sometimes accompanied me when I visited our aunt. Mid-mornings, after he and cousin Troy had finished cutting the small lawn with the push mower, they returned to the front porch to cool off. They came squeezing me out of the porch swing where I sat lazily, waiting for the mailman, who—mysteriously—walked, and who even came upon my aunt's porch, putting her mail into a dinky little box.

Once I was spread-eagle against the wall, frozen in fear, Bill and Troy began swinging, pumping the wooden porch swing. They rose higher and higher, grinning like skunks eating cabbage, barely missing the supports behind them, almost glazing the ceiling. Then all of a sudden they yelled and bailed out, landing simultaneously near the opposite end of the porch; miraculously escaping death, I thought. They were up and at it again in no time flat, however. Sailing high, then jumping out, over and over, until Aunt Margaret came to the door, double-dog-daring them to do it any-more, lest she tell Doc when he came home that night.

I've sat many a'time on my Granny's front porch, sat there listening to her rhymes or her wisdom, helping her shell peas or enjoying some of her delicious ginger teacakes. Seemed she was always serving some of her famous teacakes out on that porch beside the dusty gravel road, serving teacakes to whoever hap-pened to be traveling that countryside hungry. And there seemed to always be someone.

One day it'd be the Raleigh man, peddling the liniment Granny b'lieved in; the next day Aunt Lula'd come, selling Blair. Sometimes more exotic visitors passed the time of day on Granny's front porch, visiting, eating her teacakes. Like the time the gypsies in their

covered-wagon caravan came through, selling
trinkets and jewelry. Granny wasn't much for
fancy stuff but she did buy some new celluloid
hair pins, some more pins for putting her long
silver hair into a bun.

And another time a feller with the first
compact, portable Victrola I'd ever seen stopped
by Granny's 'piazza', as my Aunt Essie sometimes laughingly called it. Passed out some
little books about the judgement of God, turned
a crank to wind the contraption, and then
played a record with a weird-sounding sermon
on it. Granny was her usual patient, accommodating self. She let him say his spiel, even
though it was against what she believed, being
grounded as she was in God's Word and knowing that it taught that faith in Jesus Christ—
his death and resurrection—and confession of
one's sins, was the only thing that would save
a body's soul from Hell.

Granny even gave the man a glass of cold
water from the well and some of her fresh
teacakes. Lastly she quoted a little scripture
from the Holy Bible, and ventured that she's
gonna pray that God'd open his eyes to the
truth. Then she mentioned that she figured
Old Bossy's bag was about to bust and the calf

was prob'ly having co'nipshun fits to be let in
to its mama for a while. The feller packed up
and left. Later when Granny shared the whole
business with my folks I heard Mama say,
"Why, that's an unadulterated heathen doc-
trine, not believing in Hell's fire."

The tenant-farming houses where we lived
when I was young were never located near
shady streets nor even main country roads;
they were hidden away, as if the folks who'd
built them were ashamed for the world to see.
Being located as they were, however—at the
end of little roads— whenever we were sitting
on the front porch and someone arrived we
didn't have to wonder if they "just happened
by." We knew for a fact that they had come to
visit US, OUR FAMILY.

The folks who came to our porch were,
most often, the Watkins' dealer, or the insurance man. And on Sunday afternoons—in all
seasons except the winter—the neighbors or
the kinfolks came. For that reason one of the
early Sunday morning chores was a thorough
sweeping of the porch. And if a stray chicken
had wandered thereon and left "a pile" late on
Saturday afternoon, then a scrubbing was in
order also. The task was lightened, however,

enjoying the morning glories that ran up and down on the twine Mama'd trained them on, fancying up the porch.

When the neighboring men paused out front to visit with Daddy they usually seemed reluctant to come up on the porch and sit in a straight chair. Instead they would begin their conversations by just propping one foot onto a door step, resting an elbow on their elevated knee and placing that hand underneath their chin. After a few minutes they would either sit on the doorstep, the edge of the porch, or sort of squat down on their hunches beside the porch, ever talking. And after each change of position my Mama and Daddy would begin, anew, insisting that the visitor "Come on up, make yourself at home and sit a spell." But the menfolk seemed to always reply, "Naaaaa, this'll do. I can't langer long; be time fer chores t'reckly."

As much as I cherish the memories made on others' porches and formed on our own when friends and extended family were present, my prized times are those when our immediate family sat alone on our little unpainted, often-rotting, front porches. Lolled there on Sunday afternoons with Daddy's lanky frame stretched out, his head resting on the back of an up-turned straight chair. And him either snoozing or reading the Bible. Mama reading also, God's Word or the Country Gentleman Magazine. Or her busy picking the dead leaves and bugs off the potted plants which framed the porch. Plants from cuttings borrowed of others, then growing in rusty syrup buckets and leaky chamber pots.

Bill would be pouring over a Lash LaRue Western Comic book about the man in black with the bull whip. Studious Frances would be reading in her literature book. Others of us would be playing with the paper dolls cut from the cattylog, inhaling deeply of the peach and apple blossoms, or the crepe myrtles, from the yard's edge.

Our back porch was different, it was an even more casual place. Back there we had a wide shelf and a broken looking glass nailed to the wall. When coming from the field all tired and dusty we stopped by that shelf for a drink of water, to wash our hands and face, and comb our hair before noon meals.

We could do other things on the back porch which were unthinkable on the front one. Out back we could shuck a mess of corn without standing in the rain; the silks could be swept off later. We could feed the baby kittens a bowl of buttermilk and watch their little frowned-up-faces. We could even leave the slop jar, the chamber pot if you please, on the back porch —just for a few minutes. That is, if an emergency arose as we brought it from the pasture where it has sunned all day. Not in a million years could we ever walk around front with, much less set down the chamber pot on the front porch.

Our front porch served it's greatest value on hot summer nights as we sat there as a family in the deepening dusk, swatting mosquitoes,trying to rest from the day's hard labor while waiting for the house with it's hot tin roof to cool enough so we could sleep inside. During these times we listened to the hoot owls, and screaming hyenas. Daddy'd whistle to the whippoorwill and fool him, and call one up, to the very edge of the porch.

Today I, like most folks, do not have a front porch, nor a back one. The coming of air-conditioning, TV, and rampant crime has seen to that. My "porch" is only a stoop, a place to pause without the rain while I unlock my door. And most folks today who have a "porch" at all call it, instead, a patio. They use it for grilling burgers, then rush inside quickly to eat in cool comfort. Or else they have a sun-drenched deck, a place on which to stretch themselves and sun bathe. No longer are porches a place to sit and play checkers with grandpa, a late afternoon location for daddies to tell stories to their families. My husband and I are two who are saddened over the loss of porches; over the decline of the mid-way places, if you please, between the great out-of-doors and the close-ness of inside. But our hearts are broken most of all over the Passing of the faithful old Porch Sitters.

Granny's Teacakes Mellowing In A Flour Sack

As we come to the teacake and cookie section I wax very sentimental—remembering my Granny Porter's teacakes, and my Mama's cookies as we rushed in from school. And thinking back to my own kitchen—when the hum of the afternoon school bus meshed with the opening oven door as I took up hot cookies to welcome my three precious children—Greg, Glenda, and Glenn—into the love and safety of home. It is only fitting that this division begin with a touching poem.

THE COOKIE JAR

Submitted by Grace Barrett, Westminster, S.C.

A house should have a cookie jar for when it's
        half past three
And children hurry home from school as hungry
        as can be.
There's nothing quite so splendid as spicy, fluffy
        ginger cakes and sweet milk in a cup.
A house should have a Mother waiting with a hug

No matter what a boy brings home—a puppy or a bug
For children never loiter when the bell rings to dismiss
If someone's home to greet them with a cookie and a kiss.

MY GREAT-GRANDMA'S TEACAKES

By way of Mama. Actually the teacake recipe was given, almost a century ago, to my Grandma Nancy Hocutt Shirley by a neighbor, a Mrs. Skelton, whom Mama and her siblings called Grandma Skelton.

2 fresh-laid eggs   1/2 tsp baking soda
1 tsp Watkins' vanilla*
1 1/2 tsp baking powder
2 teacups sugar   3/4 C fresh buttermilk
3 pieces of fresh, salted butter (size of egg) or
*   about 3/4 C, melted*
6-8 C flour

In a bowl beat with a wooden spoon: the eggs well, then add the sugar and mix good. Add the buttermilk, the butter (not too hot), vanilla, soda, and baking powder. Beat some more.

Sift about 6-8 C flour onto your bread tray and make a well in the center with your hands. Pour the mixture into the well and work the flour until stiff enough to roll. Roll out and cut in the size you want. Or just pinch off little pieces and form into small little cakes, using your hands. Use two sticks of stovewood for a moderate oven. Bake until lightly browned.

*My Granny Porter's teacake recipe was similar, except she mixed all of hers in a bread tray and she used about 1 tsp of ground ginger instead of the vanilla. And she pinched off pieces of the dough and rolled each cookie out, or patted it, separately, with her hands. Sometimes she added hickory nut pieces on top. Hers were the most delicious teacakes in the world. If there were any left after the first afternoon she tied them up in a clean flour sack; they mellowed, becoming more and more delicious daily.

TEACAKES (Over 100 years old)
Opal Broughton, Northport, AL

1 C butter	2 C sugar
3 eggs	3 T buttermilk
1 tsp baking soda	1/4 tsp nutmeg
6-7 cups flour	

Cream butter and sugar. Add eggs. Mix well. Dissolve soda in buttermilk and add to the above mixture. Add nutmeg. Add flour gradually until you have a stiff dough. Roll to about 1/4 inch thick and cut with cookie cutters of your choice. Bake at 375 degrees on top rack of oven.

GRANNY'S TEACAKES
Eula Burkhalter, Coker, AL

1/2 C butter	1/2 C Crisco
1 C Sugar	1 egg
1 tsp Soda	1 tsp vanilla
(Flour)	

Add all ingredients together and put just enough flour to make slightly stiff. Pinch off in little balls. Flatten with a fork. Bake at 350 degrees for about 10 minutes. Note: Not too sweet.

OLD FASHIONED TEACAKES
by Debra Edwards, Sterrett, AL
(Handed down from her Grandmother-in-law, Grandma Flora Edwards)

6 egg yolks, 2 egg whites	2 C sugar
1 C melted butter	2 T vanilla
1 tsp soda dissolved in 1 T vinegar	
Flour—6-8 C (to make a soft dough)	

Beat the eggs, then add the melted-and-cooled-butter, the soda-vinegar mixture, and

the vanilla. Stir in the sugar. Add flour to make
soft dough. Put flour on a board and pat your
ball of dough around on it. Roll thin. Cut into
rounds or desired shapes and place on a slightly
greased pan. Bake in moderate (350 degree)
oven. Debra says Grandma Edwards recom-
mended " cutting the recipe in half and I found
out it was a good idea, in terms of the exhaus-
tion factor. It takes a LONG TIME to make all
the cookies."

SCALYBARK COOKIES
Charlene Pickle, Bishopville, SC

1/2 C butter (or shortening or 1 stick oleo)
1/2 C brown sugar   1/4 C granulated sugar
1/2 tsp vanilla   1 egg
1 C flour   1/2 tsp baking soda
1/2 tsp salt
1 cup Scalybark hickory nuts or other nuts.

Cream butter and sugars. Add vanilla
and eggs. Mix dry ingredients together and add
to mixture. Drop on ungreased cookie sheet by
teaspoonsful. Bake 10 minutes at 375 degrees.

MOTHER'S SUGAR COOKIES
Edith Sweetin, Tichnor, AR

2 C sugar   1/2 C Buttermilk

4 C flour   1/4 tsp baking soda

3/4 C butter (or shortening)

2 eggs, well beaten

1 tsp nutmeg   1/4 tsp salt

Cream shortening and sugar. Add eggs. Sift flour, measure. And sift with baking soda, nutmeg and salt. Add milk alternately with dry ingredients. Mix thoroughly. Drop by teaspoonfuls onto well greased baking sheet. Bake in hot oven, 400 degrees for 10-12 minutes.

MAMA'S SOPAIPILLAS

Freda Madison, Jackson, MO

2 C flour   1 T baking powder

1/2 tsp salt   1 T lard (shortening)

1/4 tsp vanilla   2/3 C lukewarm water

Lard (or oil) for frying

Sugar/cinnamon mixture(or powdered sugar)

Stir together flour, baking powder, and salt. Cut in lard until mixture resembles cornmeal. Add vanilla and gradually add water, stirring with a fork.

Turn onto a floured surface; knead into a smooth ball. Divide dough in half; cover and let stand 10 minutes. Roll each half into a rectangle. Using a knife cut into 2 1/2 inch squares. Fry a few at a time in deep hot lard or oil, about one-half minute each side. Drain. Sprinkle with the sugar/cinnamon mixture as Freda's Mom did long ago— or roll in powdered sugar for a modern twist. Makes about 18.

Time To Dig And Hill
The Sweet 'Taters

I stopped by an old gent's farm recently; the 80-year-old was braving the last heat of summer to dig his sweet 'taters. It took me back across the years to when my Daddy was the one carefully maneuvering the plow to avoid nicking the red tubers that would be much of our winter's food.

Being the meticulous soul that he was, every few feet Daddy'd say, "Whoa, Maude!" and drive the plow to a resting position. Then he'd gently kick a nice potato or two free from their camouflaging clods of dirt. Sometimes he'd comment about the "too much rain" making them oversized and filled with cracks or the "too little rain" producing only strings. Years when they weren't perfect he'd say, "They ain't gonna be the best we've ever had but like I told your Ma, 'they'll shore beat no 'taters a'tall'."

Daddy's best quality was kindness; while plowing up the potatoes he'd often loop his reins on the plowstock and double back to help pick up—making the task easier for the troupe of us who were following the plow.

After Daddy'd finished routing the "roots" from the hard soil, he changed old Maude from the plow to the ground slide (which had been fitted with the sideboards to accommodate lots of potatoes with each trip). As he pulled along- side the piles we children loaded them for their ride to the "hill." When the slide was filled to capacity, Daddy'd lovingly pick up little "Dick" and plop him on top of the pile, saying, "How about a ride, Square (Squire) Skimp?" (And later Mama'd have to rub kerosene on the seat of "Dick's" pants to remove the sticky residue left by the potatoes.)

Some times we grew so many potatoes we took them from the field in our wagon's bed. But the year that Bill and I killed most of the young potato slips wasn't one of those bounti- ful seasons. The following is my confession:

As an introduction let me explain. Some farmers bought their young sweet potato plants, by the hundred, from the feed store in town; we grew our plants "from scratch."

About March the seed potatoes were "bed-ded down" in a plot of well-pulverized soil in a sunny location. Daddy placed the seed pota-toes about as close together as my cousins and I slept when Aunt Lula and her big bunch came and we made down pallets for the night. But instead of having to fight for warm cover as we did while we slept—the potatoes were covered bountifully, with stable fertilizer which made them go through a heat and begin sprouting quickly.

Now there were two methods for setting out the slips after they were cautiously sepa-rated from the mother potatoes in the bed. The first step for both plans included someone dropping the slips, two to three feet apart, on top of elevated rows. If the ground was soft and wet the easy method could then be used—that of carefully placing an old hoe handle onto the end of the slips' roots and gently pushing them downward into the soil. One final little jab with the stick would fill the hole with dirt and you could then move onward, planting the next slip.

The second method—which had to be used when the soil was hard—was tedious, dirty, and back-breaking. With it, holes had to be dug with a hoe. A dipper of water had to be poured into each hole and the slips had to be set by hand—sort of like making a big field full of mud pies, only you didn't have time to stop for any mud-pie tea parties.

The year that we had a skimpy potato crop was the one that Mama entrusted the planting of the slips solely to Bill and I. Although the ground was dry and hard as a rock, my brother and I wanted to have time for play. So we substituted Method I for Method II. In other words, we snapped the roots off many of the little slips in the harsh planting process. Others died for lack of water before Mama discovered our sin and put us to toting water, non-stop, from the spring.

But at every summer's end we hilled the potatoes up in back of the crib, on the highest, best-drained spot available.

As preparation for "the hill" the soil was made into a mound, elevating the location even more. Straw was then piled atop the soil. The potatoes were next placed thereon and covered with additional straw. Corn stalks, pointing skyward tepee-fashion, were then erected over the potatoes. Dirt was lastly thrown atop the stalks to complete the potato "hill." The potatoes were then as snug as a baby on a winter's night, protected within from the rain and the cold.

The temperature inside the 'hill' was just right for the potatoes to sweeten their juices for the cooler months. During winter one of us children was sent almost daily to remove padding from a designated "hole," reach inside, and take potatoes. We then had to carefully return "the door" of dirt and straw to shut out the weather.

When I recently saw the old gent harvesting his potato crop my mouth began to water. I thought of the sugary-sweet potatoes Mama served—baked in the stove's oven—served hot on freezing nights. I thought also of the sweet potatoes we baked in a pile of hot ashes pulled to the side of the hearth as we sat around the fireplace some cold winter nights. I remembered the fried sweet potatoes for a quick supper meal; the sweet potato cobblers for a Sunday dinner. And the best treat of all— Granny's grated sweet 'tater pies made with sugar and lots of ginger. Just the memories made me glad that it was time to dig and hill the sweet 'taters once again.

'By Guess And By Gosh' Cooking: Sweet 'Tater Pies And Sweet 'Tater Puddin's

Sweet potatoes were when I was growing up, and still are, such an important staple in the diet of Southerners until I am according it an entire section all its own. It is a delicious addition to almost any meal, yet more importantly for me, it is a memory food. Hence the foregoing story.

Whenever Mama would start scrubbing up a big pan of sweet 'taters to bake or grating some raw ones for a 'tater puddin' she'd sing the old folk ditty: "Sweet 'tater pie, and a sweet 'tater puddin', give it all away jest to hug Sally Goodin." Or if she made up lots of potato pies and we had them—to my great delight, several days straight running—well then Mama'd half recite-half sing,

> "For supper we had 'tater pie,
> For breakfast we had cold 'tater pie,
> For dinner we had cold 'tater pie,
> I thought to my soul I would die,
> Just a'eatin' that cold 'tater pie."

MOM'S SWEET POTATO COBBLER

Vera Woods, Northport, AL

1/2 C butter (1 stick oleo)	2 C sugar
2 C water	1/3 C milk
2 C sliced sweet potatoes	l tsp cinnamon
l tsp vanilla	1/2 tsp nutmeg

(Pastry for cobbler, slightly modernized)

1 1/2 C self-rising flour
1/2 C lard or shortening
water sufficient to make smooth shortening

Add shortening to flour. Work with hands until grainy. Add water until smooth. Roll out dough to 1/4 inch thick. Cut in strips. Heat oven to 350 degrees. Melt butter in a 13 x 9 x 2 inch baking dish. Peel, slice about 1/2 inch thick, and boil the potatoes in a saucepan with sugar and water until they begin to tender. Place the potatoes in the buttered pan. Sprinkle with spices and vanilla. Place the pastry strips onto the potatoes. Pour the "juice" from the potatoes over the mixture. Bake 55-60 minutes in the 350 degree oven, until golden brown.

MOTHER'S SWEET POTATO PIE
Reita Walker, formerly of Palmetto, AL

Cook 1 medium sweet potato for each pie desired. (Or, in today's rushed world, use 1 small can of sweet potatoes for 1 pie; 29 oz. can for 2 pies.) Peel potatoes. Slice crosswise, cook until tender. Drain, then mash good.

Add: pinch of salt; 1/4 C butter (or 1/2 stick oleo), 3/4 cup sugar, 1/2 cup milk, 2 tablespoons flour, 1 egg, 1 teaspoon vanilla for each pie. Pour in unbaked pie shell. Bake at 425 degrees for 15 minutes. Then at 350 degrees, until a knife will come out clean (about 40 min.).

SWEET POTATO PUDDING
Mattie Burkhalter, Coker, AL

4 C grated sweet potatoes
Grated rind of 1 lemon

Grated rind of 1/3 orange	2 eggs, beaten
1/2 C brown sugar	1/2 tsp cinnamon
1/2 C molasses	1/2 tsp nutmeg
2/3 C milk	1/2 tsp cloves

1/2 C melted butter

Mix the grated sweet potatoes, lemon and orange peel. Beat eggs and sugar together and stir into potato mixture, then add spices. Add molasses, milk, and butter. Mix thoroughly and put into buttered 2-qt. casserole dish. Bake at 325 degrees for 1 hour. Makes 8 servings.

If you are interested in making the sweet potato pudding above and have no grater, listen up. From Merle Peppenhorst of Thomasville, AL comes a solution. Many, many years ago her Mama made a grater by punching nail holes in a piece of tin, then humped it and nailed it to a board. As of 1994, after many decades of use, they still have the homemade grater in the family. She regrets she has no recipe from her Mama to send, but added, "Mama cooked using the 'by guess and by gosh' method; and her food was yummy just the same. To make a sweet potato pudding she would grate as many 'taters as she thought would fill a large biscuit pan, add whatever amount of sugar and syrup and eggs and spices she wanted to, and cook it in the wood stove oven, stirring it occasionally, until it began to get crispy at the edges. That was some sort of good eating! When cooking foods Mama didn't skimp on fat, either. If she had butter, she used it, if not, lard would do."

SWEET POTATO PONE
Jane Sellers, Brookwood, AL
Handed down from her mother, Aquilla
Lawless

6 medium sweet potatoes, grated coarsely
1 C sugar   *1 C molasses*
3 eggs   *Cinnamon or allspice to taste*

Mix all ingredients in saucepan and cook over low to medium heat until potatoes taste done, stirring constantly. Pour into greased loaf pan. Let cool. Slice and serve.

CANDIED SWEET POTATOES

My Mama could cook good, and still does so at times, but she never could hold a candle to my Aunt Gertrude Porter when it came to making candied sweet potatoes. I think it was because Mama never had enough sugar to turn them into candy the way Aunt "Gert" did. Following is a recipe I've developed after several discussions with my Aunt about her unwritten way of preparing the delicacy.

6-8 medium sized sweet potatoes, peeled and

cut into wedges, about 6 wedges per potato.

3 C granulated sugar   *1 C brown sugar*
1 C butter or 2 sticks oleo   *1 T vanilla*
1/2 C water

Into one very large oblong pan/dish or two medium ones place the sugars, oleo, vanilla and water. Heat slowly on stove eye, melting the butter and dissolving the sugar. Spread mixture evenly over the pan/pans and lay the potato wedges thereon, spooning some of the mixture on top and permitting it to drizzle down. Place into 400 degree oven, center rack, and bake approximately 1 hour. Turn the potatoes (carefully with a spatula, to avoid breaking) every 15 minutes, permitting alternate sides to first soak in the syrupy mixture and then to brown somewhat.

The potatoes will shrink as they cook, and the syrup will cook down low. Aunt Gertrude recommends sprinkling additional white sugar atop the potatoes near the cycle's end; it promotes browning. (Sometimes I start out cooking in two dishes and toward the end pour all the shriveled 'taters into one pan for the sake of having only one dish that gets "really messed up by the syrup popping and baking on the sides near the end of the cooking time.") This does, indeed, mess up an oven, and a baking dish-but, my, my—the candied potato wedges are out of this world! I think if I did not have them for Thanksgiving and Christmas meals my children would not even bother to come home.

My Life'd Never Been The Same Without Fruit Jars

When John Mason patented a "threaded-top glass container for the home canning of fresh fruits and vegetables" in 1858 he could never have imagined how it would change life for millions. And many of the more than 100 billion jars made since that time have popped in and out of my life's saga.

The freezer boxes and the Dazey Seal-a-Meals now taking the place of glass jars can never give the sense of security, the beauty, nor the pride that once filled homemakers' hearts at seeing shelves upon shelves of filled Mason jars ready to see their families through the winter months. I recall how Mama would stand and marvel at her canned goods in the pantry— at the beauty of the huge orange Alberta peaches, canned in halves, shining brightly through the jars. Or the purple Indian peaches, pickled. And the brilliant green of the beans.

My Mama, like many others, travailed over the canning of the contents of these jars. And then on frigid nights she fussed over the jars the way she did over her babies—wrapping them in every spare old quilt, snuggling them down against the chance of freezing, spewing up in icicles, and bursting open, spilling their precious contents onto the rough wooden floors.

We used the pint jars for jelly and jam, and for drinking water from—or milk, when all the jelly glasses were chipped. And for drinking iced tea on the Fourth of July when Aunt Jessie, Uncle Earl, and their three boys came to visit and we got a block of ice from town. Once dinner was finished, the jars provided our music—we tapped on them with our tin forks; sounds high and low, little water or lots in the fruit jars.

My brother Bill'd run home for lunch on freezing days and bring back six-year-old-me a pint of hot soup in a Mason Jar. And I'd crumble my cornbread into the jar and eat it in the cloakroom up at Zion when I was in first grade. The smaller jars were also filled with freshly churned butter on hot days and taken down to the spring to float around in the cold water in the wooden box, getting the butter firm, while the milk chilled nearby in the large, half-gallon jars. How could we have ever enjoyed these things without the fruit jars?

We'd take a half-gallon to the rolling store and get it filled with kerosene for just a nickel. And when the kerosene had been emptied into lamps we'd keep the dusting rag in the jar, closing in the kerosene odor and the dampness of the rag for later use as well.

Grains of corn were put into a Mason Jar at school for the Halloween carnival. For only a copper you could place a guess on the number of grains therein and stand a chance of winning a box of water colors or a new pocketknife.

The jars were used for all sorts of things—to keep things in and to keep things out. We sealed our dried fruit therein during particularly rainy winters; it prevented mold and worms from stealing our fried pies. We canned the preserves for our Christmas fruitcake in them. And when rationed sugar was turned into caramel or chocolate fudge in early December it was hidden in the bottom of Mama's trunk. Once placed there in quart fruit jars it kept little hands off until Santa's big night.

We put honey from the bee tree Daddy robbed down by the spring—put the honey into all shapes and sizes of jars; just squished it in, honeycomb and all. The jars—I felt as a kid—kept the bees from coming and taking the honey back. Our choice cantaloupe, water-melon, and pea seeds were also safe inside the glass jars—safe from dampness that would make them sprout early, and safe from hungry mice.

In the sparse years of my childhood any-thing really valuable was dropped into a clean fruit jar and stood upon the mantel shelf—the little locket Aunt Margaret once gave me went there. And so did the pennies we were saving to buy the baby some new shoes. But Daddy's false teeth, in their jar, were kept nights on the kitchen window sill.

On Decoration Day the white cane and the climbing baby roses were cut and arranged in a fruit jar—the prettiest one we owned, the blue jar; arranged and placed on Little Robert's tiny grave. Other days we cut old maids or poppies from the front yard and put them on the doily on Mama's Singer machine; they, too, looked lovely in the blue fruit jar.

We took water to the field in the gallon glass containers and buried it in the sand to keep it cool; or buried it in the cotton on the wagon. When we worked the far field and couldn't come home for lunch Mama arose with the chickens and cooked our vegetables. Potatoes were taken in one fruit jar; cabbage packed into another, and corn bread was sliced and put into yet others; the food was secure in them, safe from the pesky ants.

When a young bull yearling was killed, the beef was canned in jars for preservation. And if a hog was killed late in the spring—and my folks feared the weather was too hot for it to keep good—well, then sausage was fried up and canned also. After hominy was made in the winter we filled jars with it and shared it with our neighbors.

With all of those special uses for the fruit jars it is no wonder that sadness surrounded our family when the fire died down around the big black pot, disclosing that several of the filled jars therein had worked away from their protective "quilt" and had broken during the out-of-doors four-hour-waterbath-canning of the beans. We didn't have the money to buy more of the jars (which early had cost only five, six cents apiece, complete with caps and rubber seals).

When the jars broke I even repented that I had complained so much about having to wash them in tubs of water with old dead bugs and spiders. My friend Buna tells how she cried when she lost many, many quarts of corn PLUS the treasured fruitjars. Her husband had helped her with the dreadful chore, a'goin' over to the field and a'gatherin' a full wagon load of the good corn. Then together they shucked, silked, cut off and even pre-cooked dishpans full of the good corn. But the kind neighbor who had brought her new-fangled pressure cooker over to help Buna can the corn quickly—well, she didn't really know how to work the gismo. And Buna certainly didn't. Cooker after cooker of the corn they took from the stove and opened, only to have the lids pop off—or the entire jars to explode. Determined to get it right, they kept on trying. Only after they'd ruined about 70 quarts of corn plus the fruitjars—days later someone told them the trouble was "they'd failed to let the pressure drop before opening up the Pressure Canner's lid. A miracle they hadn't been scalded or cut to death themselves with flying glass." They had saved, then lost, a long cold winter's worth of corn in one ill-fated day.

Yes, the valuable fruit jars were long ago hoarded; passed down—among our ranks—from one generation to the next, like precious china and silver is inherited among the rich. At times a family's wealth was even measured in the "fruitjars" it possesed. Gertrude Sanford, a dear older friend, tells that once a neighbor died and left her an inheritance of 300 fruit jars. She was outside, excitedly washing them, when a feller happened by, commenting, "If you fill all those jars this year, you're gonna have to put sand in some uv 'em." But—by jingoes—Mrs. Sanford worked like a Trojan and made it; it was like the year my Mama and our bunch canned more'n a thousand quarts uv foodstuffs.

With our lives back then almost "hanging by a jar," as it were, it was no wonder we cried when they broke. But if they just chipped around the top—that was a different matter. My brother Bill and I didn't cry when that happened. We knew—with them no longer good for canning—we'd be permitted to take those jars underneath the high pillars of the back porch where we had our "log road and highway".... Under there we used the chipped jars for cars, and rolling stores and for log trucks; we had a great time pretending with them. My life...I promise you...would just NEVER have been the same without the wonderful glass fruit jars. Thank you, Mr. Mason—and Mr. Ball.

I'm Thankful For Red Rover And Granny Gray

Crisscrossing the land these days I marvel that children are seldom seen outside, playing carefree in woods and yards. It reminds me to give thanks for the childhood and youth I knew, one where parents and other adults permitted us to play as hard as we worked.

A child of three spent hours every day running, "riding" astride a hobby horse when I was young. The mothers sewed little cloth horse heads to attach to old sticks for the kiddoes. Growing older, the youngsters graduated into pushing a syrup-bucket-lid attached to a stick. Life was good when you could run barefoot up the road, with your little push toy fairly flying—round and round, ahead of you. Go around the curve and out of sight, to meet the mailman or the school bus. And know that when you got a little older you could roll an old car tire like your eight-year-old brother, could balance and run with a 'caisson.' Or have fun with a little wire hoop and a metal wheel for rolling.

Come Sunday afternoons we kids would really be seen outside, be seen and heard like an army, playing together with friends and cousins, from toddlers to twenty-year-olds.

Divided into two teams we would huddle, thinking up some good action to portray, like "gathering corn." One team would rush up to the line, stand there and say "BOMB, BOMB, BOMB, Here We Come." The waiting group would ask, "Where're You From?" The first would chorus, "Little White House Just Over The Hill." Again would come an inquiry, "What's Your Trade?" And the reply, "Lemonade." Then the demand was issued, "Well, Get To Work And Get It Made."

The first team would fly into action, pantomiming the "gathering of corn." The tall fellers would be yanking the ears of corn off the high stalks. Someone would be driving the team of mules along, pulling the wagon. Even the smallest fry would do their part, pretending to be picking up the ears of corn which had fallen to the ground.

The work continued as the second team guessed, "Picking cotton!" "NO." " Gathering muscadines!" "NO." Then when they guessed, "Gathering corn!" the working team had to be ready to fly, to speed back to their home base. Anyone who was tagged by the opposing team while attempting to return home—that individual had to go to the other side to play.

It then became the second team's turn to act out something, like "killing hogs" or "making a playhouse." Back and forth we played, exercising our minds, our bodies, learning the give-and-take of playtime, of being patient with the littlest ones.

After a while we would decide to play "Antle (Ante) Over." Again there would be two teams, plus a string ball involved. The teams would position themselves, one in front of the house, the other behind it. The team with the ball would yell, "Antle Over," throw the ball over the housetop, and head out running, trying to make it safely to the other side of the house without being tagged by the oncoming team. The opposing team would grab the ball and head around the house, trying to tag as many of the oncoming players for their own as possible.

The trick to the number one team reaching the other side in safety lay in throwing their opponent off as to which side of the house they would be approaching from. However, when the house was held high off the ground with stacks of old rocks like ours was, this was impossible. The other team kept peeping under the house, watching for their approach. But we had great fun playing the game, nonetheless—and the exercise ensured none of us ever were overweight.

Another game in which all ages combined was " Red Rover, Red Rover." When choosing up teams we tried to even things out—some strong, some medium, some little folks. The teams lined up in the sandy, grass-free yard. One group called out, "Red Rover, Red Rover, let Nonie Faye come over." (You see, they knew I was a weakling and couldn't damage their ranks.) I would size up the situation, look for the weakest link in the line of folks who were facing me, hands locked. Then I would head out, run my fastest, and throw all my weight against two held-tight hands, hoping to burst them apart. If I succeeded I could choose one of the two to take back to my line, a sort of prisoner-of-war, an addition to our team.

The opposing team then daringly called out, "Red Rover, Red Rover, let Bill come over!" The big boys on the team were eager for an encounter with my strong brother, were anxious to prove the two strongest could hold the line against him, for indeed he would accept the dare and run into the toughest part, the "brick wall."

Eventually the big boys would grow restless for some sure-enough "hard ball," if you please. Sometimes they would ride those motorless, brakeless truck wagons down the death-defying, curving hills or go at breakneck speeds on the flying jennies. Other days they would choose to play Crack-the-Whip, which could be as dangerous to the boy on the end who got whipped off as the running of the bulls in Spain. Tug-of-War wasn't exactly child's play either, with the strong fellers lining up on either side of a line drawn in the sand. One sudden jerk on the grass rope by the opposite side could send boys cascading on top of one another, or could burn the hide from the palms of their hands.

The favorite "tough sport" of the boys seemed to be "fighting" down by the hog pen with big acorns. Or to saunter out to the barn and gather ammunition for Corn Cob Fights. They would pile up huge piles of cobs, leftovers from the mules' meals. And they would begin the battle, throwing the cobs with all the strength of their muscles built by removing huge stones and stumps from the new ground.

Usually the corn cob fights were just fun. But, occasionally—if Bill felt Bob had reneged on the rules they'd set, Bill'd "get his dander up." And then you'd better watch out— especially if you saw him double his tongue up and stick it out of his mouth just a tad, biting down on it with his teeth. 'Cause then he was, for sure, gonna dead-eye a big, soggy cob into Bob's head. "WOW," what a headache! But at least there were no guns involved and any animosity felt was soon relieved; the boys always parted as good friends. And any "drug deals" encountered, when those gangs got together, were limited to a little "smoking of rabbit toback'r" out there behind the barn.

The girls and small boys chose less strenuous games while the big boys made war. We jumped rope, played "London Bridge is Falling Down" or "Granny Gray, can I go out to play?"

I still remember being Granny and saying, "No, my child, I'm afraid you'll stay." The other answered, "No I won't." Then I came back, "Yes you will." Again, "No I won't." I then repeated my lines, "Then take three licks and get away." I would then administer 3 tiny licks with a teensy switch and the child would run to hide as I called out, "But don't get into granny's corn crib."

After all the 'children' were sent out with such licks and admonitions, I'd begin the searching. "Children, where are you?" The reply would come back, "We can't hear you!" I would say, "I'm sending the goats after you." Then, "I'm sending the pigs after you." Finally I yelled, "Then I'm coming to get you myself." The children then came rushing from all directions, running, trying to make it "home" before I, Granny Gray, caught them. The one who was caught became Granny Gray and the fun continued.

In the "Good Old Days" my siblings, friends, and I enjoyed these active outdoor games with our parents' permission and blessing. With the exception of the corn cob fights we played them during school recess as well. And now, as I pause and ponder, counting my blessings, I give thanks that I was not a TV nor a video child but rather that I had these wonderful experiences in my early life.

Granny's Hikker-Nut Cake 'Made' Christmas

Granny's hikker nut cake MADE Christmas when I was a kid. Oh to be sure, there were other treats: the cedar Christmas tree hung with popcorn strings; the peppermint sticks, the chocolate drops, and the orange sneaked in from the Yellow Front by our 'Santa Daddy,' plus the re-cycled dollie clothed by Mama's patient fingers. But I remember when Granny's hikker nut cake was indeed the highlight of the festive season. It, especially, made the poverty I knew seem distant and unreal.

Stacked today beside ultra-rich tortes and fancy desserts Granny's little Christmas cake probably wouldn't seem like much. Maybe even back then the simple sweet wasn't the tastiest around. Would've lost out to Aunt Beck Hannah's dried-apple-stack-cake or to a Bessie Cake— one of the pound cakes made famous by the dear old black lady, Bessie, who lived in the edge of Granny's yard one year. However, my proof of Granny's 'pudding,' I now realize, wasn't in the eating, but in the making.

Early in the fall every year Granny's kith and kin would begin to tote hikker nuts up to her house. We would gather them in our bonnets, our hats, or our tied-up apron-pockets; gather them whenever we passed through woods, whenever we walked underneath huge hickory trees enroute to fields, to pastures, or to wash places down by the springs. We'd gladly be on the lookout for the chance to scoop up a handful of the scaly-barks and bring them for her joy; her use in teacakes or a hikker nut cake for Christmas.

Our Granny Porter was a tiny, magical lady, "no bigger'n a wash rag 'n a bar uv soap," some said. Always had a small bun—made from long silver hair—fastened on the back of her head by means of wondrous celluloid combs. She wouldn't qualify in the least for "Today's Corporate Woman" 'cause she was never in a hurry, never rushing to and fro. Yet Granny always seemed to accomplish the important things in life.

When I was five we lived "just out the lane" from Granny. And Mama'd let me skip, run, and hop out there many 'a morning as the older kids went to catch the school bus. Let me excitedly go to spend the day with Granny. And thus it came to be that I was —that year— included in the making of Granny's Christmas hikker nut cake.

For days on end we'd sit, just Granny and me, sit by the fireside picking out the cracked hikker nuts with a tiny nail or a metal hair pin. Picking out the "nut meats" as some folks called 'em— but me and Granny, we just called 'em "hikker nuts." We'd put the tiny little pieces —which she taught me to patiently pry from the many partitions of the hard nuts— put them into little bowls on our laps. It didn't bother me that the bowls filled slowly 'cause the whole time we'uz pickin' Granny'd be off in her memories, telling me some grand stories and I'd be lost in the wonderment of 'em. The slow grind didn't seem to pester Granny any, either— maybe 'cause she had me to listen.

Sometimes Granny'd tell sad stories about

how her maw'd lost four babies in one day, lost
'em in death to colitis, "that terrable thang
what nobody knew a sangle remedy fer." Then
after awhile she'd talk, kinda under her breath,
shaking her head, about a friend who'uz "living with a drunkerd fer a husband, who'se
meaner'n a snake to'er." I felt all grown up
when Granny'd talk to me like't another woman,
saying, "Law, law, I tell ye, living troubles is a
heap worse'n dead troubles."

I would, occasionally, interrupt Granny
to ask when we were gonna make the hikker
nut cake and she'd smile and say, "OOoooh,
it'll be a few more days, Chile. We gotta git a
heap more hikker nuts picked out, and some
good fresh eggs, and plenty'a butter from Ole
Bossy 'fore we commence."

I didn't get upset 'cause bout that time
Granny'd hobble into the kitchen, saying something about her rheumatism, and come back
with a sugar-biscuit for me to nibble while she
talked on. Telling about somebody "who'se
almost eaten alive by a panther one morning
when she went out to milk. Fannie 'lowed the
panther had killed and eaten the calf and was
sitting on the lot gate, picking it's teeth,"
Granny passed down.

Before long my daddy's maw'd do her sing-song of "Jumped Up 'Fore Jay Break." By cake baking time she'd taught me the entire poem about a feller getting up before day-break, putting on his boot-shoes, taking his shotgun and jumping on his mule, his jackass. About him going to the cotton patch and killing a bunch of buzzards and later salting them down in his Mama's old soap goard. Here it is:

"Jumped up 'fore jay break, Pulled on my boot-
    shoes,
Jerked down my got shon, Jumped on my jass
    act,
Loped down the patton cotch, Killed a buck 'a
    tussards.
Salt'em down in Mam's old goat soarb
Behind the staddar fox."

The morning I arrived at Granny's all bundled up in my big coat and head rag to find her letting a cake of butter 'warm up' on the hearth in her big mixing bowl, I knew THE DAY had arrived. Pretty soon she began creaming the butter with a big wooden spoon, something unusual for Granny. You see, Granny mixed all her biscuits and even her teacakes in her bread tray, using her hands instead of a spoon. When the sugar and butter was as smooth

as silk that morning Granny sat it on the
kitchen table, put on her bonnet, threw a
shawl around her shoulders and announced,
"Come on, Chile, we've gotta git some real fresh
eggs fer that Christmas cake."

Even on the way to the hen house Granny
had time for me. When I begged, "Granny, can
we draw chickens in the sand?", she obliged.
Taking a stick she stooped over, then began
drawing in the smooth sand. First a little
circular head, next a larger oval body, two
straight lines for legs—connecting to three,
four equally straight, but short, lines for toes
on either foot. A triangular beak, lines for a
tail, and a little ridgy-comb up top finished it
off. Except for the one round dot of an eye—
which Granny insisted I make.

After I clapped my hands in wonder at the
sight, Granny suggested "I" draw some little
doodies to go with the mama hen. Then, still
bending her small frame over—now to cradle
me— she placed her hands on the stick next to
mine and guided as, together, we drew a whole
passel of baby chickens in the wind-swept
sand of Granny's yard.

Granny took her straw broom and
brushed up the kitchen floor once the precious

cake was finished; I stood admiring it sitting proud in her pie safe. The Plain Cake layers (page 109) had been covered between and again on top—with the sugar-butter-sweetmilk icing (page 111) which just sorta disappeared into the cake, except for cementing the piles and piles of hikker nut pieces into place.

The cleaning Granny gave the kitchen was needed. While she had let me help with the mixing and the stacking I had spilled flour, sugar, then dropped one egg. While sprinkling the nuts I scattered them all over creation. When I'd started to cry at my clumsiness, Granny just smiled and patted me, saying, "Aw, pshaw, Chile, don't streak yer pretty face. I can allez git another egg, or more flour, but they's just one sweet you."

Christmas arrived in a few days. Whenever kinfolks stopped in to see Granny she'd go to the pie safe, take out the hikker nut cake and insist they enjoy a delicious slice of it. Then before each left for home she'd walk to her big yellow chifferobe, take out her worn purse and—from the pension which resulted from her son Sam's death during WW I—from her skimpy means she would happily parcel out to each and every one, a one-dollar bill.

I was tickled pink to get a dollar for Christmas when I was five; during the Depression a dollar lasted a long time for a kid. But even more lasting have been the joys, the memories of being with Granny, the time for learning her heart, for feeling her love as she and I together made her Christmas Hikker Nut Cake.

And now has come the wondrous blessing from my Savior and my Lord, Jesus Christ— the joy of writing this, my Book No. 4, for you. My only regret is that I couldn't include all of the wonderful recipes you dear folks sent; perhaps they'll be in a Book No. 5. But for now I'm thankful for the opportunity to team once more with my dear sister and illustrator, Trillie Brown, to bring you these special stories and memory foods in GRANNY'S TEACAKES, GRAB'LED 'TATERS, AND A GILLION TWICE-TOLD TALES.